Strings Attached

A Sam Dunne Mystery

AIRSHIP 27 PRODUCTIONS

Strings Attached
© 2022 Fred Adams Jr.

Published by Airship 27 Productions
www.airship27.com
www.airship27hangar.com

Interior illustrations © 2022 Sam Salas
Cover illustration © 2022 Rob Davis

Editor: Ron Fortier
Associate Editor: Steve Bennett
Marketing and Promotions Manager: Michael Vance
Production and design by Rob Davis.

ISBN: 978-1-953589-37-8

Printed in the United States of America

10 9 8 7 6 5 4 3 2 1

Fred Adams Jr.

People say that when someone dies, a story ends. Sometimes, when someone dies, a whole new one begins.

Any time I get something in an envelope from an attorney, I always think about it before I open it. Most times it means trouble or at least a headache; divorce papers to sign, some new wrinkle on a lawsuit, or just a big question mark—what now?

The envelope was addressed to Samuel Dunne. Not my usual Sam, Samuel, like my mother called me when I was in hot water. The return address read Herbert Weintraub, Attorney-at-Law with an address in Sharpton. I didn't recognize the name, but I knew the town. I drove through it every time I went to the Lewisburg State Penitentiary.

I guess I should explain that. I'm Sam Dunne, guitarist, vocalist, songwriter, and part-time English Prof. There are a few standard jokes people throw at musicians, like "don't quit your day job," and "an amateur musician has a full-time job; a professional musician has a wife with a full-time job." I have neither. What I have besides an education in the Hard Knocks School is a Master's degree in English Letters. I fill in the gaps in my music income by teaching classes at Hanniston Area Community College, known locally by its acronym, as in, "Do you go to college? No, I go to HACC."

Once in a while, I'm offered an off-campus class, usually Comp I or Business Writing at some factory or hospital as a perk for the employees or in an attempt to improve their personnel. Once, I got to teach Creative Writing. Walter Creighton, an English Department fossil normally teaches it, since he has three self-published books of poetry in print, but he passed on this one. The class was for convicts in the Lewisburg Federal Prison. I initially wasn't crazy about the idea, but I had bills to pay, so I took it.

I climbed the stairs to my apartment on the third floor. I quit using the elevator when my belt threatened to cut me in half. I was fumbling with my keys when my girlfriend Carlotta opened the door. She stood on tiptoe and kissed me before stepping back to let me inside.

She was wrapped in a white terry cloth robe that contrasted her dark curly hair, still damp from the shower. "Notice anything?"

That's a loaded question from any woman to any man. Get it wrong,

5

and you could be sleeping on the sofa for a week. I looked around the room and saw nothing new. I took a shot. "New shampoo. Smells great, C." I was the only person on the planet allowed to call Carlotta anything but her full name, and that was a long time in the works.

"Good guess." She gave me a mischievous grin but didn't tell me whether I got it right. "You need a haircut, Sam."

"Too depressing. Every time I get one, my hair looks a little thinner and a few more gray ones show up."

"At least it matches your beard. The day you start with the comb-overs, like those little-olds at the diner, I'm packing my bags. Anything interesting in the mail?"

I handed her the other odds and ends and kept the envelope from Weintraub. I stared at it while she sifted through the bills, junk mail, and beg letters from a half dozen charities.

"Are you going to open that, or just stand there staring at it all day?" Carlotta nudged me with an elbow.

"I'm studying the envelope for clues as to whether it's bad news or good news."

"Shrodinger's Subpoena?" For a person who calls herself a "career waitress," Carlotta is exceptionally well-read and has a wit like a razor blade. She moved in with me two years ago after we met in Myrtle Beach. I said I had no wife. Carlotta is worth at least two of those.

"They have to deliver them personally. They can't send subpoenas by mail."

"See? Mystery solved." She gave me her "don't be an idiot" look out of the tops of her eyes. "Just open the damned thing, Sam. Get it over with."

"I can't help thinking it's like Pandora's Box." I turned the envelope over in my hands. "Oh, what the hell." I tore open the envelope and all but ripped off the end of the letter inside. The letterhead matched the name and address on the envelope. "Mr. Dunne:" it began in a businesslike fashion. "You have been named sole beneficiary in the Last Will and Testament of my late client Bolton Robert Watts."

Boley Watts. I knew the old blues man was dead, heard about it when I was playing a week-long stand in Atlanta, and it upset me that I couldn't make it to the funeral in the penitentiary graveyard. I heard nobody was there but the chaplain and the grave digger. I guess I was the only friend Boley had the last year or so he was alive, but I never expected he'd leave me anything. For that matter, I didn't think he had anything to leave.

Let me tell you about Boley.

▌▌

Boley Watts was known for two things, playing the Blues and robbing banks.

He told me he was born Bolton Robert Watts in a coal patch south of Pittsburgh in the mid-forties and grew up around the mines, mills, and coke ovens of Southwestern Pennsylvania. "It never got black at night," he said. "Them coke ovens painted the sky orange. I got so used to the sulfur smell from the coke works over the hill, first time I smelled clean air, I thought something was wrong."

He learned how to play guitar from his uncle and put the skill to good use. "I started playing in bars and strip clubs when I was fourteen, had the clap by the time I was fifteen, and by the time I was draft age, I was a sideman for Penny Boy Whitford and playing blues joints all over the South. Two years in the Army, and I was back on the street with a guitar case in my hand and a head full of songs nobody ever heard. But I was determined they would."

Boley's signature sound emerged because of the size of his hands. He was a big man to begin with, but his hands looked like they belonged to a giant. "I had trouble fitting those thick fingers of mine between the frets, so I bought a twelve-string guitar for the wider neck and put a pair of pickups on it. I strung it with the regular six strings, then I got the idea to double up the A and low E for more bottom." He added a copper pick to the mix, and the result was a snarl as dark and mysterious as a midnight bayou.

King Snake Records hired him as a studio musician, and in the early years of Rhythm and Blues Boley's guitar growled from radios all over the country. His big break came when Florence Makem didn't show for a recording session. "I say, 'We got the people, we got the tape. Let's record something,' and I launched into 'Ready Betty.' Everybody else jumped in, and when I looked through the glass into the booth, I saw them big tape wheels turning and I knew I was rolling along with them." The session went on, Black Snake put him on his own vinyl, and the Race Music stations put him on the air.

For two or three years, in the early days of Rhythm and Blues, Boley Watts was a name; maybe not as big as Chuck Berry or Bo Diddley or Muddy Waters, but he was halfway up the ladder and playing the best clubs and theaters across the South. "I wasn't exactly a king, but the princes had nothin' on me."

Then the British invaded.

Boley told me once, "Them Beatles and Rolling Stones and all yanked the rug out from under me and a lot of good blues men, and they did it playin' our music. My contract runs out, and Black Snake tells me they don't want to record a new album. They tell me, you cut a demo, bring it in ready to press, and we'll give it a listen." He snorted. "Give it a listen. I made those boys some money, maybe not as much as Chuck or Muddy, but enough to not be tossed out like last week's newspapers. I decided I'd show them all.

"Things then wasn't like now. You couldn't record an LP in your living room with a computer and a microphone. You needed a studio, you needed side men, and most of all you needed money."

That led Boley to his old friend Rufus Small. "Rufe was always a bad boy. Seemed he knew a hundred ways to make a living without ever working a day. I told him I needed money and how much I needed, and he said, 'No problem.'

"Rufe introduced me to his partner, Elton Suggs, a white man, and one of the most evil sons-of-bitches I ever saw. He couldn't have been taller than five feet, but he was one of those guys had a cold eye, cut your throat for a dime and laugh about it. Rufe and he cooked up a scheme and put me in the middle of it. Rufe said, 'We'll just stick up a bank,' like as if he was saying we'll just walk downtown and buy some cigars."

"I told my wife, Martha, I was goin' to do a week in Little Rock, and we was on the road."

The first bank the three robbed was in a mid-sized city just over the Pennsylvania border in Maryland. "We hit that bank in Cumberland, slick as you please. Waltzed in guns out and ran out the door with all the cash from the drawers. Problem was, after we split three ways, there wasn't enough for what I needed to do. So I had to do it again.

"The next bank was in Pittsburgh on the South Side. I remember the name, The Iron and Glass Bank. We came in the same as last time, wearing turtlenecked sweaters pulled up over our faces. I was holding a gun on the customers, and my shirt slipped down and one of them says, 'Ain't you Boley Watts?' Knew me from my album covers, I guess. Took me by surprise, and I just froze. Elton grabbed the money, and Rufe grabbed me, and we hightailed it out of there."

Thinking ahead, Suggs had booked a pair of rooms in a hotel in Uniontown, fifty miles south of Pittsburgh, close enough to the borders of

West Virginia and Maryland that they could be out of the state in fifteen minutes. "We holed up there for three days while the cops ran around in circles hunting us. The papers never mentioned me by name, so I figured I was safe."

"'One more job,' Rufe said, 'and we'll be set for a while.' There were three banks in Uniontown, one of them a block away from the hotel, and that's the one Rufe decided to hit. The plan was to drive off like we were headed for the border, switch cars, then double back into town to hide in the hotel while the cops ran all over Hell's half acre looking for us.

"So we walked into the First National Bank of Uniontown, and Rufe got brave and did something he didn't do before. Instead of just taking the drawer money, he took the cashier back into the safe and made him fill up the bag like trick-or-treat on Halloween. I was driving 'cause Rufe didn't want to risk someone recognizing me again, and about the time he and Elton came running out of the bank, the alarm bell went off. There was a cop half a block away, and he came running. Elton shot him and he fell on the sidewalk.

"Two miles out of town, we traded the car for an old pickup truck Elton stole and stashed in a broke down barn. We pulled coveralls over our suits put on painter's hats and spattered our hands with white house paint. The truck had a ladder and some empty paint cans in the back, and if anyone saw us, they'd think we were just three working stiffs. We got back to the hotel an hour later, tallied up the loot, and called room service for steaks and beer."

The plan worked. For two days, the trio hid in the hotel room, watching the news on television. Part of the loot was a bundle of cash held in escrow for a big sewage project that upped the ante to a reported hundred twenty thousand dollars. "The cops figured we were out of state and out of their reach, but what we didn't figure was that robbing that bank in Maryland and coming back to Pennsylvania made the case federal, and here come the FBI. That put a whole new face on things, then to make matters worse, the cop Elton shot died in the hospital.

"'We can't just split up the cash and take off,' Rufe said. He tore the wrapper off a packet of twenties and laid them out on the coffee table like a dealer playing blackjack. 'These sons of bitches all have sequential serial numbers. We spend one of them, and the FBI gonna know where we are.'

"'So what do we do?' Elton said.

"'I know some people who'll trade old bills for these at eighty cents on the dollar.'

"'What they gonna do with them?'

"'Take them to Mexico, from what I hear. They want to meet us, see the money, and make a deal. We'll go tonight.'

"'What stops them from shooting us and taking it for free?'

"'I'm just bringing a sample for them to look at, one of those packets. We'll hide the rest of it someplace away from here in case they come looking. I have a few ideas.'"

What they didn't know was the bellhop they'd been sending out for bottles of Kasser's 51 and cigarettes figured out they were the robbers and dimed them to the law.

"That night a little after one in the morning, Rufe and Elton and I climbed into the pickup and got about a block away from the hotel when lights come on, cars come from every direction, and the truck was blocked in. I heard a voice on a bull horn say, 'Po-lice. Get out the vehicle hands in the air.'"

Elton pulled his pistol and every cop on the street emptied his gun into the pickup.

"I shut my eyes and covered my head with my arms thinkin' this is it. I'm gonna die. Then the shooting quit. Looked around and saw Elton with about twenty holes in him on one side of me, and Rufe slumped dead over the steering wheel on the other. I took inventory and saw I didn't have a scratch. And that day, brother, I located Jesus on my life map."

The packet of twenties in the First National wrapper Rufe had in his coat was enough evidence to put Boley away by association, but the Feds weren't happy with just that. They tore the rooms at the Titlow Hotel apart and couldn't find the rest of the loot. And Boley wasn't talking.

Boley Watts was beaten nearly to death by overzealous cops and agents in the local jail trying to get him to reveal where the money was hidden. His left eye drooped after that because of a shattered cheekbone, and three of his fingers were broken, one by one, two on his left hand. "The harder they hit me," he said, "the harder I dug in my heels. They coulda killed me. I wasn't sayin' nothin'."

His venture into bank robbery bought Boley 35 years in the Lewisburg State Penitentiary, where other people thought they might coerce him into telling where the loot from the last job was hidden.

"I was headin' into the showers when two cons come at me." Years of punching his way out of honky tonks had made a fighter out of Boley. The brawl was quick and vicious, leaving the attackers lying on the floor unconscious and bloody. "When the guards came a couple minutes later, I was sitting on the bench smoking one of their cigarettes. I told the guards, 'Never saw two white boys fight each other so hard. Way they fought, you'd a thought they was niggers.'"

The second try on Boley happened after his cellmate was transferred out and Boley had the cell to himself for a few days.

"Word got to me that they was comin',so after the last stand-up head count, I rigged the bottom bunk to look like I was sleepin' in it, and I hid in the top bunk against the wall so they couldn't see me. I waited, and sure enough around four o'clock, I heard the bars slide open. Thing is, they had to come through the doorway single file.

"I figured I had to hurt them as bad and as fast as I could if I wanted to get out of it alive. The first one cleared the door, and I sprung off the top bunk and landed on him, knocking him backwards into the second guy just coming through the doorway. I brought both hands down on the back of number one's neck, and he was out of the running. I grabbed the second one by the shirt and ran his head into the wall then shoved it into the toilet. Trouble was, there was three of them. I guess they learned from the last time that two wasn't enough.

"I was bent over the second man when the third ran in and shanked me in the back. I turned around and clamped one of my hands on his head and I shoved the fingers of my other hand between his teeth and dug my thumb in under his jaw. I yanked his jawbone half out of his face. He screamed, sort of, gurgling on all the blood, and fell to his knees. One good kick and he shut up.

"I pulled the dude's head out of the toilet, but it was too late. He was done breathing, and I knew right then I'd never see the outside again."

After those two attempts, word got around, and everyone gave Boley a wide berth except the penal system. Although it was arguably self-defense, killing his attacker bought Boley another fifty years with no parole, and he wasn't likely to live long enough to walk out of the iron gates on his own dime. "And you know what the real hell of it is, Dunne?" he said. "My clock would'a run out about this time next year. Ain't that some shit?"

The classroom was like any classroom anywhere if you ignore the steel security door and the bars on the windows. The problem was getting there. If you've never been in a prison, all I can say is stay out. There's no feeling in the world like walking through those steel doors and having them clang shut behind you, even if you know you aren't staying the night. The word grim doesn't even come close. The oppressive atmosphere is a shock at first, then it tones down to a general apprehension that settles into a constant third-eye awareness.

When I signed the contract to teach the class, I'd been fingerprinted, subjected to a background check, and given a list of rules that applied to all visitors. It didn't really prepare me for the experience. I've been in jail once or twice for small things like drunk and disorderly, but there is no comparison between a small-town drunk tank and a maximum security prison. From the moment it heaves into view as you drive over the hill until it disappears in your rearview mirror, every aspect of the place is designed to intimidate and oppress. From the air, if you're high enough off the ground, it almost looks like an old-time college campus. Up close on the ground, you see the white wall that encloses it. What you don't see until you go through the gate is the inner fence capped with coils of razor wire.

My first day there, I parked my van in the designated area outside the gate and emptied my pockets. I locked my watch, my wallet, my pocket knife, and everything but my car keys in the console. Not all the criminals are inside. This trip, I brought nothing with me, not even a sheet of paper to teach my class. Naked came I. I've read many times about the chilling effect of hearing that outer door slam shut behind you and the grate of the lock sliding home, but it didn't prepare me for the near sense of desperation that I was in there, and I wasn't going to leave until the Man said so.

The guards buzzed me through the entrance doors. I identified myself and they gave me a form to sign with the purpose of my visit. They cleared my entrance, and then they sent me through a full-sized metal detector like the ones the TSA uses in airports. Next, I was wanded, ordered to remove my shoes and my coat, and subjected to a full pat down by a uniformed guard the size of a steer. These boys didn't screw around. They were pleasant enough, but I was advised in advance to not even joke about security matters. No wisecracks about them missing the Glock up my ass or the C-4 in the heel of my shoe.

All this was probably unnecessary since, as I walked in, I passed a sensor the size of a fifty-cent piece mounted on the wall inside the door that scanned me for metal, explosives, and drugs.

I was given a hang tag that designated me as a visitor, and a guard escorted me to Deputy Warden Mark Haines' office for a briefing. Haines was as big as any of the guards, and his gray suit did nothing to disguise the thick muscles of his chest and shoulders. Like most of the guards, his hair was buzzed down to his scalp. Under his suit coat Haines wore a black designer T-shirt; no collar or necktie for someone to grab in a fight. A thin scar split his left eyebrow in two, making it look like a pair of wings. Haines was no appointee; he'd come up through the ranks.

"First, we appreciate your being here. We believe that education is a key factor in the rehabilitation process. The inmates in your class have earned the privilege of being there by virtue of good behavior, a privilege that can be revoked if anyone causes a problem."

"You speak the language like a native."

He grinned. "Besides an AJ degree, I minored in Sociology with a special certification in bureaucratic bullshit." Tough and intelligent and articulate. He'd be Warden someday. His smile flattened. "You have read the rule sheet, correct?"

I nodded. "It seemed comprehensive."

"It is, but I would caution you about one other thing. Make no mistake, all of our inmates are dangerous felons. We haven't had a riot here since '95, but it could happen any given day. You will find that despite their demeanor, these men are not stupid. They possess a sort of feral cunning, almost instinctive, that serves them well in here. They are as skilled and practiced at manipulation, intimidation, and prevarication as you are at your skill set. Don't allow any of them to get inside your head. You'll have one hell of a time getting them out."

Haines leaned back in his chair. "There will be at least two guards in the room at all times."

"Do I really need —"

Haines cut me off. "Yes. These men will behave themselves or lose the privilege, but many or maybe most of them live in a constant state of tension. A wrong word, a wrong look, a sense of disrespect could blow the lid off any one of them. I'm not saying that you would cause a situation, but you will be in the room if one erupts." He pushed a button on the com box and a uniformed guard came in. He was wearing a navy blue jumpsuit with a velcroed belt and embroidered badge. No hardware on the uniform. His name tag read Carlson. "Let's go, Mr. Dunne."

Haines and Carlson led me through a series of corridors, gates, and doors so convoluted that I expected the Minotaur to pop out any second. We entered a sort of hub area that branched into several rooms from a round central console manned by guards watching video monitors that showed every room in the area from several angles. We walked halfway around the hub and down a short corridor. "Here's your classroom."

The classroom was everything I expected; institutional chrome and Formica school desks bolted to the floor (no talking circles in this class) a table and chair for me, no lectern, and concrete block walls with windows near the ceiling that gave the feeling of being in a cellar. The walls were painted institutional green, that sickly shade that's supposed to have a calming effect on prisoners and students. They must have a lot in common.

A guard was already in the room, and my supplies were on the table. A sheaf of plain white paper, and a handful of rubber pencils. The inmates were permitted nothing that could be used as a weapon. The shafts of the pencils were flexible, as was the center core, what in an ordinary pencil would be graphite. I tried one and found it wrote like a crayon. No paper clips, clamps, or staples were allowed. I decided it was probably a bad idea to joke about paper cuts, too.

The door opened, and the blue-clad students filed in, each patted down as he entered the room. Apparently the indignity was the price of admission. In a moment, I was being stared down by twelve violent criminals. I stared back.

Haines said, "Men, this is Sam Dunne your instructor." He nodded to me, he and walked out of the room, and the door closed behind them, leaving me on the wrong side of the bars in a tiger cage. One guard took a position beside the door, the other at the back of the room. Neither sat, nor would they.

I picked up the roster sheet and called each student by name. No first names or nicknames; protocol dictated that I call them Mr. And last name. No exceptions. "If I say your name wrong, correct me now, or I'll be saying it wrong the whole semester." I learned early in my teaching career that identifying people as individuals from the start is a plus. I couldn't imagine anything more embarrassing than an instructor asking a question six weeks into a semester and pointing to a student raising a hand and saying, "Uh, uh—you." It was an issue of respect between teacher and student and with cons, that was a big issue.

Body language. Half of the class sat upright, arms folded across their chests. The other half slumped insouciantly in their desks as if they were short on bones.

"I'm Sam Dunne," I said. "A little bit about me. I have a Master's Degree from Ohio State, and I have some experience in Creative Writing. I'm a singer-songwriter—"

"Gin Sing," Terrence Mitchell, a slim guy with a ferret face said."You wrote 'Cold Fire.'" Mitchell knew his oldies.

I nodded. "Yeah, I played for Gin Sing a few years back."

"You capped Danny Barton."

No sense denying that I had killed my former bandmate. "Yeah, I did."

"Dude, you need one of these." Jesse Bohna, a behemoth with a shaved head and a thick curly black beard pointed to the corner of his eye where two teardrop tattoos were inked into his skin.

"Naah," said Mitchell. "He didn't murder anybody. It was self-defense, right, Dunne?"

"That was the verdict, Mr. Mitchell."

"I still say you oughta get the teardrop."

I didn't tell him that I actually qualified for two of them. "Why advertise? I'd rather it be a surprise."

Everyone laughed. I looked around the room and saw faces that told me I was suddenly one of the club.

"You a songwriter?" The speaker was a black man, one of two in the room, sitting in the back row. He wore heavy-framed glasses that didn't hide his drooping left eye. I scanned the roster. Bolton Watts. His hair and full beard were the color of iron filings. "What a skinny white boy gonna teach me about writin' the blues?" Then it hit me. Bolton. Boley. "Eight-String" Boley Watts the blues man was in my classroom.

I rose to the challenge. "Not a god damned thing, Mr. Watts."

Boley stiffened in his desk. "What you say?"

Nobody breathed for a minute. The guards stiffened a little too.

"I can't teach you to be creative. I'm going to sharpen the tools you have and show you a few you haven't seen before to make it go smoother."

Boley eyed me over the top of his glasses. "We see about that, Sam Dunne."

I gave it a three count and handed each of the students a sheet of paper and a pencil. A few bent them double, laughing. "Looks like your pecker, Wally," one said. Another jibed, "Naah, it's too long."

"I need to see how you write," I said, "so today, you're going to write me a paragraph or two."

"What about?" Paul Benaducci (I just knew his goombahs had to call him Paulie) said.

"Glad you asked. Here's your subject: if you could change your name, what name would you choose for yourself, and why do you think it would suit you better than the one you have?"

"Any name?" Benaducci said.

"Any name."

"What if we like the name we have?" Mitchell said.

"Then what if you had to change your name? Give yourself an alias."

Mitchell nodded, and everyone went to work.

At the end of the class, they filed out, being patted down yet again.

I threaded the maze in reverse with a guard at my elbow, collected my car keys, and walked out of the prison. I was relieved to be out of there, but I shared an understanding with those guys who pull weekends in jail for DUI and know that next week, they'll be going back into the maw of the monster.

That night, I read the paragraphs. The spelling was average, the grammar was poor, and for the most part the punctuation was missing in action. Boley Watts' mechanics weren't much better than the rest, but a sharp wit burned through the bad writing.

"Bolton Robert Watts - named after my grandpa, but that ain't no name for a blues man. Sound like one of them butlers in an old black and white movie where the black people wear fancy clothes and do all the work for white people wearing fancier clothes. Been called Boley all my life 'cept when Mamma was mad, then I was Bolton Robert and knew I better hide my ass. There's three things that make a blues man a good name: the Bible, sex, and drugs. If I had to give myself a new name, I'd call myself Jeremiah Johnson Jones. Triple J—smokin' all the way."

I laughed out loud, and when I read it to Carlotta, so did she.

IV

As the term continued, I introduced the class to the nuts and bolts of poetry. When Donnie Black sneered, "Poetry's for fags," I quoted Lovelace: "Stone walls do not a prison make, nor iron bars a cage."

"Huh?"

"By the poet Richard Lovelace, written to his fiancée Althea, Mister Black. Or how about Ezra Pound? He wrote *The Pisan Cantos* while he was locked up. He had a wife and a mistress when he was eighty. I don't think he was gay. Or maybe William Welsh?" I quoted "Grapey's" lines about watching a fellow inmate do a high dive off the third tier and split his skull on the concrete. I decided to not include Oscar Wilde's "Ballad of Reading Gaol" in case on some off chance Black knew Wilde's history. "What about song lyrics? Song lyrics are poetry as much as sonnets or sestinas, or limericks."

"What's a limerick?"

"It's a five-line rhyming poetry form. As soon as you hear one, you'll recognize it." I rattled off the infamous "Man from Nantucket" limerick, and a few others. Everybody laughed. It seemed everyone in the room knew at least one, and the inmates segued into an impromptu competition as to whose was raunchier. After the initial enthusiasm died down, I said, "Now, let's talk about rhyme and meter, what makes those poems—and they are poems—work."

After limericks, the class moved on to other basic forms. I decided to take a chance. "How about the blues, like Huttie Ledbetter, 'Leadbelly'? We have an authority on the subject with us right here."

Boley looked up from the tablet where he'd been doodling. "You the teacher, Dunne. You tell 'em. If you get it wrong, I'll let you know."

"But you've written and sung more blues songs than ever I have. I figure you know a lot more about it than I do."

"You say you can't teach people to be creative. You can't teach them to write the blues, neither, Dunne. You can tell them this many words, this rhyme with that, but if they ain't got the soul for it, it don't fly. You got to reach deep in yourself for the pain, and bring it out where you can hear it cry and moan."

He closed his eyes, took a deep breath, and started into "Clock Just Keep on Tickin".

Clock just keep on tickin'.
You ain't walkin' through my door.
Got a dire premonition;
you ain't comin' back no more."

His a capella voice filled the room with a gravelly baritone that vibrated my lungs with its power.

"I see you gettin' fancied up, say,
'What's that all about?"
You just give a cold eye, and say,
'I'm goin' out.'
I say 'Where you goin'? You say

His a capella voice filled the room...

it ain't none of my affair.
I say, 'But I love you, baby.'
You say, 'I don't care.'
Clock just keep on tickin'.
You ain't walkin' through my door.
Got a powerful suspicion;
you ain't comin' back no more."

The room was silent. Boley looked around him and said, "You can put the words on paper, but not the blues. Be like tryin' to put lightning in a bottle."

The other cons stared at him in wonder, and I realized they'd never heard him sing before.

At the end of the class, as the guards were taking the men back to their cells, I stopped Boley for a second. "Do you ever get a chance to play?"

"Ain't played for years."

"That's a damned shame. Don't they have a music program here?"

"They got a few guitars layin' around, but I can't play 'em proper. He held up a hand like a baseball mitt. Hands this size, you can't play just any guitar. Don't feel right. Don't sound right."

The guard took a step toward us to hustle Boley out of the room, and I held up a "one-second" finger. "You play a twelve-string neck with six strings, right?"

He nodded. "With double A and low E."

"I'll see what I can do."

"That'd be good, Dunne, but don't make no promises 'til you talk to the Man." He turned and followed the guard out of the room.

That night over supper, I told Carlotta about Boley.

"He sounds like an interesting character. Maybe you could interview him for an article for one of the guitar magazines, or even a book."

"That's not a bad idea. That's why I keep you on the payroll." I told her about my idea of finding a guitar for Boley to play in Lewisburg.

"I don't know much about jail," she said, spearing a shrimp from her salad."Do they allow people to have their own stuff?"

"I guess they do. He said they have a few instruments available, but they wouldn't let him keep one in his cell."

"Why not?"

"For one reason, if he played it and sang, the whole block would hear him. Not everybody likes the blues. Besides, he's long-term for killing another inmate. I don't imagine they want him to have something in his cell he could convert into weapons; make a club out of the neck, a knife out of the pickguard, a garrote out of the strings."

"I can see that. Whatever goes wrong, it's the administration's ass."

"I'm going to talk to Johnny Malone. Maybe he's got something in the store I can rig for Boley to play."

"You have a good heart, Sam." Carlotta leaned over and kissed my cheek. "Just remember what the Warden said about letting people inside your head."

I laughed. "Don't worry, darlin'. Once you got inside, there wasn't any room left for anybody else."

The inmate poetry varied from funny to sad to frightening. A few wrote about women, a few wrote about death, and a few wrote about the violence and despair in the Joint. Boley was the exception. He wrote blues lyrics that were so fluid and so soulful, that they seemed to rise off the page and float around the room looking for a tune to bring them to life. Other times, they revealed a wry sense of humor, like "I Don't Understand how you Understand", a song about wifely intuition:

> When I get my paycheck if I make an extra ten,
> Tuck it in my shoe then I mosey on home again.
> You give me that fish-eye, say,
> Don't you give me none of your jive.
> I know you got extra dough,
> C'mon and give me five.

I told them when we worked with rhyme about Rod Mcuken's famous statement that nothing in the English language rhymes with the word "orange." The next class, Boley handed in a lyric titled "Ain't no rhyme for Orange."

> Ain't got a rhyme for orange, so I'll sing about a grape.
> Ain't got a rhyme for orange, so I'll sing about a grape.
> When she twines her vines around me,
> there just ain't no escape.

> Ain't got a rhyme for orange, so I'll sing about a plum.
> Like my baby sweet and juicy
> all night long til the mornin' come.

Ain't got a rhyme for orange, so I'll sing about a prune.
Even when she's old and wrinkled
Still have me howlin' at the moon.

"These lyrics are terrific," I told Carlotta. "They deserve to be put to music and recorded."

"Could you do it?"

"I could try, but I'd feel really uncomfortable. I'd be afraid of not doing them justice. They deserve Boley's touch, and he deserves the privilege of recording them."

"Have you asked the Warden about bringing a guitar in for him?"

"Not yet, but I'm hoping that if I show him what Boley's written, he'll allow it. The next step would be for me to bring in some equipment and try to record him in the prison."

"Maybe you could start a movement like Bob Dylan did for Hurricane Carter, try to get him an early release."

"One step at a time, darlin'. One step at a time."

V

Six weeks in, the next phase of the class was writing fictional narrative. What I got to learn 'bout writin' stories for?" Boley said. "I write songs."

"Yeah," I countered, "but don't your lyrics tell a story? Isn't that what the songs are about? All the same things you learn about writing fiction: character, plot, setting, theme are part of the story you put in a song: who, what, where, when, why. When you write a song, you're telling a story in verse instead of paragraphs, but knowing how it all works is a help."

When the first try at short stories came in, everybody wrote one but Boley, sort of, who gave me instead a lyric about Po'Boy Smith, a blues man who lost his career, his mind and ultimately his life over a conniving woman. I could see that what I said had some effect. His lyric was linear narrative poetry instead of a set of discrete ideas verse for verse around a basic theme. What amused me was that he wrote it in paragraph form as per the assignment, but when I read it aloud, it revealed a four-beat meter and an ABABCDCD rhyme scheme, like e e cummings used to do when he wrote sonnets. That was the day I decided to talk to Mark Haines. I have a generally bad attitude when it comes to dealing with authority, but in this case, I decided to swallow my pride and go in humble.

"What you see in front of you is unique creative genius," I told him. "Boley Watts has the potential to be a force in music again, but he can't do it without an instrument he can play."

Haines looked at his desk for a moment then raised his head and said, "You've heard of Jack Abbott?"

I could see where this was headed. "Sure, Norman Mailer's protégé. *In the Belly of the Beast.*"

"He was only out a month before he killed somebody. Then he went back into custody and ultimately killed himself."

"I'm not asking you to let him out, I'm asking you to let his creative soul out."

"I'd have to take it up with the prison board. They'll be meeting in two weeks."

"Would it help if I came on his behalf?"

"Let me broach the idea myself. I think it has some merit. Watts has behaved himself pretty well the past few years." Haines thought about it for a minute then gave a curt nod. "I'll see what I can do."

I didn't hear from Haines for three weeks. I knew better than to be a pest. That's usually a short road to No with people in authority. Then a guard handed me a note on my way in to stop in Haines' office after class. I didn't mention it to Boley, deciding to wait for the results of the meeting. After the class was over, a guard escorted me to the Admin section. When I came through Haines' door, he was talking with an older man in a dark suit and tie. "Sam, meet Warden Darren Grayson."

The warden rose and turned to shake my hand. He was a small man, but every detail of him from the shine on his shoes to the hard set of his jaw broadcast power over men's lives. His grip was unyielding but not as bone-crushing as Haines' handshake. Here was a man who didn't have to show off to let you know he was in charge.

"Mr. Dunne, I've reviewed your request with Mark and with the Prison Board. I am wary of the long-term consequences setting a precedent for bringing objects and devices into the prison. Today, it's a guitar. Next month, who knows what? And the first time we said no after saying yes, the lawsuits would begin."

I tried to keep a poker face, but I knew that my disappointment must have shown. "That is unfortunate." Don't argue, I thought, it'll just make it tougher on Boley in the long run.

"However," Grayson went on, "Mark has suggested an alternative that may work without causing us headaches. I am going to reassign Bolton Watts from the prison laundry to the carpentry shop. He'll work the same shift and load as the other inmates, but he will also be allowed to work on a project of his own, as others have been from time to time. Building a guitar is not out of the question."

"If he can do the woodwork, I can supply the hardware he'd need to finish the job, with your permission and supervision, of course."

"Mark can work out the details with you. I admit I am curious as to what will come of this. I believe in rehabilitation, even for inmates who have no hope of release. They still have to function in prison society, and anything that makes that function easier for all concerned is worth exploring." He rose. "You have one more session, I believe."

"Yes, sir. Next week."

"I think your class has had a positive impact on some of the participants. That also weighed in my decision. Are you willing to follow this through after the class has ended?"

"Yes, sir. I want Boley to play again."

"I have to ask; what's in it for you?"

"Nothing in particular beyond the satisfaction at seeing that talent doesn't go to waste."

Grayson peered into my eyes, and I felt as if he were looking into my skull and checking for hidden agendas. "I believe you, Mr. Dunne. Good luck."

That afternoon, when Carlotta came home from Dora's, I told her the news.

"Sam that's great." She put her arms around my neck. "I'm proud of you. You could have walked away from that class and never thought about him again, but you're giving Boley a chance."

"Ladders," I said.

"What?"

"Grayson and Haines are giving Boley a ladder—like Andrew Carnegie said, you don't give people handouts, you give them ladders, as metaphor for the tools and opportunities to improve themselves and climb to new heights. Don't give Boley a guitar, give him a ladder that he can use to raise himself. Building his own guitar will give him a stake in whatever he achieves."

"Sounds like the Warden's a smart man."

No argument there.

VI

The final class meeting, I decided to take a chance and asked the students to each read what they thought was their best work from the class. I say take a chance because one thing I left out of the classroom protocol to that point was peer review. I was afraid that if someone bared his soul in a poem or story and it was met with derision, there could be bloodshed, in the classroom or later, for the perceived disrespect. Waiting until the end was a good idea, it turned out, because the class had become something of a bonding agent for them. All understood now what went into writing a piece of creative work and they respected others' efforts.

When I walked into the room, I saw Boley sitting in his usual desk at the back of the room, but for the first time, he was smiling. He nodded to me and went back to scribbling on his tablet.

At the end of the class, I told my students, "Now you've seen what you can do with words. Don't stop writing. Every poem, every story is a unique expression of personal genius. It would be a disgraceful waste of talent if any of you never picked up a pencil again to put your thoughts on paper."

At the end of the class as the men filed out, Boley stopped. "You fixed things good, Dunne. You give me a chance. I owe you."

"What you owe me, Boley, is music. You have lyrics. Soon you'll have a guitar. Write the songs."

Boley gave me a somber nod and walked out the door.

VII

I stayed in touch with him after the class ended. I never gave Boley my telephone number, and he never asked for it. Instead, we corresponded by mail, since inmate access to computers and e-mail were severely restricted, and cell phones for texting were forbidden. I went several times on visiting day to sit on the other side of the plexiglass divider and listen to Boley tell his stories. I decided that Carlotta's idea was a good one; I would gather material from Boley and maybe do a biography. Boley liked the idea. I guess he knew instinctively that the only two ways a man gains immortality in any culture are through his descendants and through the tales of his people, and since he had no children—"leastways none I ever knew about"—he saw a biography as a way to live forever.

He talked about bands, women, and honky tonks, and nights when he had to punch his way out of one joint or another, and the night when he met Martha. "I's singin' 'Hoodoo Woman,' and I get to the line where I say, 'You got me under your lovin' spell, gonna send me to heaven or send me to hell?' and I look out in the crowd, and everything else just went out of focus but that woman's eyes.

"She divorced me a year after I went up, but I understand that. I didn't even mind that she took up with my cousin Billy St. John. The thing she did that was the lowest blow, though, was she sold every one of my guitars. Didn't leave me one. For that, I can never forgive her. She might as well'a cut off my dick."

Boley even talked about the bank robberies once or twice. He told me how they planned them, about the "recognition moment" in the Iron and Glass Bank, and the shootout that left his partners riddled with bullets and him untouched. But he only mentioned the missing loot once. "I never told where it's at, and I ain't tellin' now. I figured that was my retirement money once I did my time. Now I know I ain't never gettin' out of here, but hell, Martha left me, I got no sons or daughters to leave it to. I figure if I take the secret with me, I'll still have the last laugh on the law."

"Aren't you afraid somebody else might find it?" I asked.

"They ain't yet, and you know how I know?" He chuckled. "'Cause them sequential serial numbers ain't never popped up on some FBI computer. I'd'a heard, even in here. Them Feds woulda come here to rub my nose in it. No, Dunne, that money's still safe as in a bank—safer."

Every time I'd visit him, Boley would give me a progress report on the guitar he was building in the carpentry shop and the songs he was writing around lyrics from the creative writing class. "That class kicked me in my backside, got me thinkin' and writin' again." I asked him how he could compose without an instrument. "I just whistle the tune, then I sing the words." I knew he couldn't read or write standard music notation, but he had an answer for that too. "I know where the notes are on the guitar, so I write down the fret numbers on the lines—what you call that? Tablature? I got it all."

When I'd ask Boley about the guitar, he'd say, "She comin'. She comin' along." One visit he told me, "Got the neck the way I want it. Had to read up on it. Took me some ciphering to figure where they go, but it's time for the frets." Then it was time for the tuners. "Don't need no nut," he told me.

"Traded two packs of cigarettes to one of the kitchen trusties. He gimme a beef bone I can shape on the bench grinder."

Six months into the project, Boley told me, "Time for the 'lectronics."

As I was about to leave, Boley said, "Hey, Dunne."

Yeah, Boley?"

"It's a good thing you writin' down what I tell you. My memory ain't good's it used to be. Sometimes I forget places, people, details, you know. You keep writin' it down so's it don't get lost."

I bought a pair of single-coil humbucking pickups and a simple three-way selection switch. They had to go through the same protocol as every piece I'd sent him, particularly the electronic components. But finally, nine months after he began, he was finished. "I decided to call her Baby," he said with a chuckle, "since she took nine months to get here." He held a photograph against the divider. Baby might not win any design contests, but I could see that Boley had built himself a formidable instrument.

Baby's body was a double cutaway Boley had fashioned from a slab of oak he found in a dusty corner of the shop. The horns were rounded and scooped to accommodate his huge hands playing high on the fretboard. The general shape of the body was asymetrical, as if someone pulled a rectangle from two rounded corners. Its finish was black lacquer buffed to what Boley called a "Cadillac shine." The chrome-capped pickups were parallel but angled high end toward the bridge to keep a lid on the doubled strings. The two knobs were simple chromed dials on the pots and the pickup switch rode just above them. Boley didn't want a manufactured bridge. He said he'd make his own, and he did, hand carved from the same bone as the nut. "I could find a guitar with a wide neck, but I could never find one with a bridge that spread the strings right, so I made my own."

The neck was hand carved from a piece of maple. And the fretboard was dark rosewood. The head looked like a Gibson design but ended in a crown. The finishing touch was the pickguard, shaped like the guitar's body from a piece of buffed aluminum.

"She's beautiful, Boley. You got to be proud."

"What I'm most proud of, Dunne, is how she sounds. I get to play her once a week in the music room. Just wait 'til you hear her."

That would take some doing. I was batting a thousand so far where the Warden was concerned, but that was allowing Boley to build a guitar under supervision in the carpentry shop. It would be a whole other game for me to be allowed in where he could play the guitar for me. I submitted my request in writing to Mark Haines with the pitch that Boley had made enormous creative strides over the past year and that it would be a shameful waste of his talent to allow his songs to go unheard. I had learned from my previous negotiations with the Prison Board to horse trade, to ask for more than I really wanted, and their compromise would likely give me the bare essentials.

I asked to bring in a pair of recording techs with a digital deck and good-quality microphones and for me to attend the session and bring my own gear to play along. What I got was a one-hour visit to the music room chaperoned by guards and a two-track Tascam recorder with a built-in mic that downloaded into a USB port. The sound quality might not be as good as I'd like, but I figured that pitched to recording execs, a demo of Boley's new material could garner support to pressure for more and better the next time.

VIII

I spent a whole day working with the mini-recorder, determining what distance, height, and angle would work best at catching both voice and guitar. The acoustics of the room would probably be lousy, concrete all around, but I had to take what I could get.

When the day came, I went through the whole drill. I had dropped off the recorder the day before to allow the prison security team to go over it completely. I suppose they wanted to make sure it wasn't made of C-4 or had an Uzi hidden in the battery compartment. It seemed foolish to me, but Carlotta was right, whatever might go wrong in there, it's the administration's ass.

The music room was a surprise. The walls were carpeted halfway up the concrete block with the same forest green commercial grade carpet as the floor. The ceiling was acoustical tile laid in a grid. An upright piano stood in one corner, and a set of drums close by. Locked steel mesh cabinets housed a few trumpets and saxophones, and similar cabinets across the room held two acoustic guitars and an old Fender Precision bass. I walked over to the piano and played a two-handed chord. I was surprised; it was in tune. I heard no blare or harsh overtones. The room would make for good sound.

The one amplifier in the room, probably intended for the bass, was an old flip-top Ampeg Porta-Flex with a fifteen-inch speaker. The guard who brought me in told me to sit in one of the chrome and plastic chairs and stay in it while he went to fetch Boley. He was gone a full twenty minutes while I counted the concrete blocks in the walls, the number of tiles in the ceiling, and the louvers in the door. I once read a description of a prison cell in which the author reduced the whole place to numerical values; height, length, and width, thickness of the concrete underfoot, the dimensions of the wire-glass pane in the cell door, and the number of tiles on the floor. I suppose if you're in for a stretch, you spend a lot of time thinking about exactly what's holding you in.

Overhead, a bad fluorescent light buzzed like an angry bumble bee. I'd have to ask it be turned off. The switches were outside the room to prevent inmates from plunging it into darkness for some bad purpose. I was gaining a new appreciation of the term 'stir crazy' when the door opened and Boley came in holding Baby in his arms like a father with a newborn child.

Behind Boley came the guards and a trusty with my gear bag. I wanted to look at the guitar, study it, appreciate the labor of love that it represented, but we had only an hour. I said, "Let's get to it."

Boley plugged Baby into that old Ampeg while I set up the recorder. I slipped a pair of earphones over my head and tapped the mic. Boley quickly tuned Baby and we were ready to roll. "Before you play each song, Boley, give me the name of the tune and say a little something about it. We're on the clock. If you make a mistake, just keep rolling."

Boley nodded. "This song called 'Tossin' Through the Night'; it's about a woman I knew down in Memphis keep me up nights thinkin' about her."

He strummed a bass-heavy E chord, tapped a four-count with his foot, and started up a quick lead line in a syncopated shuffle rhythm that traded single notes on the bottom strings with open chords. His copper pick scratched and scraped and dug a feral growl out of the low strings and a chime-like ring from the high ones, walking the fence between hell and heaven.

I can't sleep at night busy thinkin' 'bout your love.
The glory of you, woman, outshine the stars above.
Yeah, I'm tossin' through the night, girl, 'cause you the one I'm dreamin' of.

I checked the indicators and saw the light bars dancing up and down.

The sound through the headset was clear. I pulled the ear piece from one side so I could listen to the raw sound. The combination of Boley, Baby, and that vintage amplifier produced something magical and unique. Boley ended the song with a blistering top to bottom riff, looked up at me over his glasses, and said, "We okay, Dunne?"

I gave him a thumbs up. He nodded and said, "This one's called 'Three Live Rounds'; Ain't nothin' to say about it. Song speaks for itself." Boley strummed a chord and tweaked the tuning on one string. His foot tapped again, and he launched a sinuous chord riff counterpointed by those thick buzz-saw notes from the double-E.

Three live rounds in the chamber, three bullets in my gun.
Got three live ones in the chamber, three bullets in my gun.
That fool you been seein', he's gettin' number one.

Three verses in, he did a stop and switched from shuffle to straight fours while he ran a single note riff down the neck for two measures then segued seamlessly back into the shuffle tempo while his hands slid all over Baby's neck, double-stopping and catching chords on the off-beat, all the time, keeping that steady pulse from down below. I'd heard him do it before on old LPs, but never with the force and fluidity I heard that day. It was as if the guitar and he had fused into one entity, the work of his hands freeing his soul.

At one point, I saw Mark Haines' face looking through the glass pane in the door. I nodded and gave him a thumbs-up. He returned the nod but was otherwise noncommittal.

The hour was nearly over when Boley said, "One more tune. "Call it 'Top Thirteen'. It pretty much says it all for me." He set down the pick and started slapping what John Howard Griffin in *Black Like Me* called a "visceral" bump-and-grind rhythm with his thumb on the lower strings while his fingers coaxed dirty seventh chords out of the upper three.

When I been drinkin' I ain't myself
Tend to take my common sense, put it on a shelf.
You see me settin' with my whiskey by my side,
Put your hands on my bottle, them Four Horsemen gonna ride.
I might not be the meanest thing you ever seen,
But I can guarantee I fall somewhere in the top thirteen.

When I'm talkin' to women, don't you come messin' round
Spoutin' all your jive trash, try to put me down.
You think 'cause you're a younger man, that make you a better lover.
Them women ain't gonna read your book once I rip off the cover.
I might not be the meanest thing you ever seen,
But I can guarantee I fall somewhere in the top thirteen.

When I play my guitar and I start to sing,
I don't brook no interference. It's a spiritual kind of thing.
Don't go hoot and hollerin' when I start to sing the blues,
Or your friends gonna drag you outta here by your shiny shoes.
I might not be the meanest thing you ever seen,
But I can guarantee I fall somewhere in the top thirteen.

"And like the man say, 'that's all, folks.'"

"Time to go, Mr. Watts," the guard said, all business. Boley strummed Baby one last time, reached over to shut off the amplifier, and unplugged the guitar. He stood, again cradling Baby in his arms. "See you on Visitor's Day, Dunne."

"Count on it."

The guard told me again to sit in the chair and wait. This time, I didn't count the tiles, I put the headphones back on my ears and listened to what I'd recorded. The time I spent preparing with the Tascam paid off. The recording wasn't CD quality, but the words and music came through clear, and with a little tweaking on the computer, I could remove the steady hiss of the air circulator from the background and the 60-cycle hum you get from any household outlet. I decided no reverb. Just let Boley's sound speak for itself with all the raw power of the twelve-song session.

In the back of my head, I knew it was foolish, but I couldn't help making plans for Boley's future.

Back at my apartment, I listened to the raw recording again. I knew it was going to be a poor second to hearing Boley Watts play and sing live, but it wasn't as what I feared it might be. The compression factor in the internal

…and listened to what I'd recorded.

microphone flattened things down and in a maddeningly egalitarian way tried to make the volume of all things equal. The result included, among other things, the ramping up of the background noise, including the hiss of the air exchanger under the windows. I could sample the hiss and remove it, but it also took bands from the graphic EQ and made Boley's voice sound as if he were singing with his head in a cardboard box. So much for quick solutions.

I returned to the original mono track for the first song, "Tossin' through the Night" and pasted four copies of it into side-by-side tracks in the software. That way, I could make changes in one track that would be more subtle in the overall mix. Then came hours of lowering this, raising that, and erasing dead space to reduce ambient noise. Carlotta came home in the middle of all this and could see my frustration.

"What's giving you trouble, Sam?"

"I'm trying to pull the best sound out of this song, and I just can't get it right."

"How long have you been at it?"

"Since you left this morning."

"All on one song?"

I nodded.

"Maybe that's your problem. Let me make a suggestion. Take a break for a half hour and go to the next one. Work on it a while, then go to the track after that. Don't obsess on one song and burn yourself out."

I was stunned. I realized she was absolutely right. I needed to think of the session first as a whole, not as its parts. I took her advice and sat in my recliner with a wet washcloth over my eyes, which were aching from staring at the computer screen. I drifted off to sleep and by the time I woke up, the cool cloth and my eyelids were the same temperature. I could smell Carlotta's cooking and hear her humming Sonny Rollins' "St. Thomas" as she puttered at the stove. "Hey, Grandpa, what's for supper?" I said in a faux hillbilly imitation of the Hee Haw gang, one of our standing jokes.

"*Pate de foie gras,*" she shot back in a dead-on copy of Julia Child, "over grits."

"Yum yum!"

"Actually, it's cheeseburgers."

"Oh, you vixen." I levered myself out of the chair and when I took the cloth from my eyes, my vision was blurry. I looked at the clock but couldn't see the numbers. "What time is it? How long did I sleep?"

"Five-thirty, and probably not enough."

I came up behind her and kissed her on the neck. She stepped back and eyed me up and down. "Supper can wait. Go take a shower. I'm not sure I can eat across the table from you the way look right now."

I saluted. "Yes, Ma'am." I started for the bathroom and stopped in the doorway. "Would you love me more if I were sensible?"

"I don't know. I've never seen sensible. Go take your shower."

After supper, I tried Carlotta's suggestion. I shouldn't have been surprised that it was effective. There's a pragmatism to her that cuts through bullshit like Alexander's sword through the Gordian Knot. Moving song to song gave me a better feel for the totality of the recording, and as I adjusted one, I slowly learned what would work for them all. At the end of two days, I had what represented probably the best sound I was going to get.

I called my friend Cotton Breakiron, front man of the jazz trio Sax to the Max, and invited him over for a beer and an opinion. He listened to the whole set of songs without comment, and when the last one ended, he said, "That's some righteous shit, man. The brother knows what he's up to."

"I agree."

"I'd maybe give it a little touch of reverb—just a matter of personal taste, mind you—but if Mancini can't sell that to some label, the Blues is dead."

The next phase was setting all of the songs on paper, lead sheets to submit for copyright. Otherwise, the first time one of these songs was broadcast or played in public, Boley's rights and his control over the material would be at risk. I've used Finale since since the software was first released in the nineties, and it's always served me well.

There's a certain difficulty in capturing the tune of any blues song on paper. The slurred notes between a sixth and minor seventh or a major and minor third in the scale make you scratch your head and wonder, this note or that note. In the end a rigid chart is a poor stepchild to the fluid performance with all its expression and nuance.

Online copyright registration is a lot easier than the old days, but to make sure, once I registered it, I put the materials on a blind page attached to my promo website. The content could then be legally proven to be in my hands by a given date, in case anyone tried to steal the material before I had the copyright papers in my hands.

I was in Atlanta playing a weeklong gig at Harvey's Pub when Carlotta called me with the message that Boley died of a heart attack. I hung up the phone thinking it was too late for Boley, but not for his music.

I called the number on Weintraub's stationery the day after his letter arrived. When I identified myself, his secretary said that Mr. Weintraub would meet with me in his Lewisburg office the following Tuesday. When the day came, I found the address on a side street between a bakery and a Qwik-Print shop. I looked through the glass in the door and saw an empty reception desk. I pushed the doorbell button in the door jamb and hoped it wasn't wired for an upstairs apartment. It was eleven in the morning, but you never know who's a day sleeper.

In a minute, a short, pudgy man in a rumpled tan suit opened the door. "Can I help you?"

"I'm Sam Dunne. I have an appointment with Herbert Weintraub."

"I am he."

I smiled. The English professor in me always appreciates the proper case in a subjective complement. The attorney was almost a head shorter than I and almost bald, but he sported a fringe of unruly gray hair that ringed three-quarters of his head like one of those olive wreaths you see on Roman senators in old movies. He wore no jewelry and kept a five-dollar digital watch with a plastic strap on his wrist. The suit looked as if it hadn't cost much more.

"Come on in." I stepped into the reception room and he closed and locked the door behind him. He led me through a door behind the empty desk into a dingy office. The carpet was frayed, the furniture was scarred, and the window blinds were missing a slat or two, giving a scenic view of a brick wall across an alley. Overhead, a fluorescent light flickered like a disco ball.

"Nice office," I said, enjoying the shabby ambiance.

Weintraub laughed. "This dump? I just keep it for show. It's a satellite I maintain for work I do for the inmates. Sometimes they come to see me for one thing or another when they get out. I don't want them to think I have much more than they do. If they saw my office in Sharpton, I'd be burgled twice a night."

The rusty spring on the swivel chair groaned when Weintraub sat at his desk. He opened a file across his blotter and put on a pair of those annoying half-glasses you see on geeks like Charles Shumer. "All right, Mr. Dunne."

"Just Sam."

"All right, Sam. Bolton Watts named you his sole heir in his will. There isn't much." He opened a desk drawer and pulled out one of those bulky manilla envelopes the prisons use when a newcomer hands in all his personal effects. I opened the flap and dumped the contents on Weintraub's desk: 137 dollars in an alligator skin wallet, a ring with three keys, a chrome Zippo cigarette lighter, a Timex watch with a gold expansion band. There was also a silver pinky ring, with a tiger eye. It was way too big for my little finger, and when I tried it on my ring finger, it was a loose fit. I saw three copper guitar picks at least a sixteenth of an inch thick. Boley had them made special. Each had a hole drilled in the top. He ran thread through them so that if he dropped his pick (which happened often enough) he could yank it back into his hand with a flick of his wrist. The last items were a Cartier fountain pen and a silver cross as long as my thumb.

"He left this for you too." Weintraub opened the closet door to the side of his desk and pulled out a large, flat cardboard box. It was tied shut with twine, so I pulled out my pocket knife and cut it away. I had a pretty good idea what was inside, but it still made my throat catch when I saw Baby, Boley's hybrid guitar in the box.

I stared at Baby and thought about the dark magic Boley conjured out of those eight strings.

"And there's one more thing." Weintraub brought a cardboard box from the closet and set it on the floor beside my chair. I opened it and saw it held the dozens of crossword magazines I'd brought for him over the past two years.

"I take it Mr. Watts was a puzzle fan," Weintraub said without looking into the box. He'd obviously been through everything before he ever wrote me the letter.

"Now, if you'll just sign this form, stating that you've taken receipt of these items." Weintraub pushed some papers across the scarred desk. I signed at all the X's, and that was the end of my association with Boley Watts, or so I thought at the time.

"Yeah. That and playing the blues were his two passions." I hesitated for a second then said, "Was there any mention in his will about the rights to his songs?"

Weintruab shook his head. "No mention, but I'll give you a photocopy of the will, and you can pursue that avenue with an attorney who knows the music business. I can recommend one or two."

"No need. I know more of them than I want to."

I thanked Weintraub and he hurried me out the front door saying something about a client meeting in Sharpton in an hour. As I was loading Baby into the back of my van, I saw Weintraub turn the corner and drive away in a navy blue Mercedes sedan.

I took Baby back to my place, along with the other things Boley left behind. When I walked in with the box under my arm, Carlotta was sitting in my ratty old recliner reading Kingsley Amis' *Lucky Jim*. She'd been working her way through my wall of books ever since she moved in with me, and I was pleased to find that she not only enjoyed good literature but she also had a critical eye and could discuss most authors with a certain degree of authority.

She rolled her eyes in mock exasperation when I came in carrying the box. "Not another guitar. Where are you going to put that one?" She twitched her head to the wall hung with guitars, basses, and other "strang thangs" as she called them. "That wall's full."

"Don't know." I set the box on the sofa and went back to the van for the crossword magazines. I opted for the elevator this trip. Someone had stuck a post-it note on the buffed steel wall over the floor buttons. It read: "This is not your private elevator. Stop using the hold button to keep it on your floor. We know who you are. Stop it or we'll report you to management." I laughed at that one. It reminded me of days when my high school principal would come on the p.a. system and say, "We know who you are. Turn yourselves in."

Under the message, somebody, probably the offender, had drawn a crude representation of a hand giving the bird. To me, that was consummate arrogance, like wearing a T-shirt that says "Piss on you," and broadcasts the message to everyone at random who sees it. I was going to tear the bottom half of the note off, but I decided, this is America; free speech rules, so I left it alone.

I brought the box in and set it on the coffee table. "What's in there?"

"Boley's crossword magazines and a few of his personal items."

She pulled one of the crossword books from the box and leafed through a few of them. "He didn't do them all in this magazine. Looks like he skipped from one to the other." She looked through other issues. "Some of them, he did only ten or so and left the others blank. The ones he did, though, are completely filled in."

"Just a way to pass the time, I guess."

"Don't throw them away. I'll do the puzzles he didn't." Carlotta is a puzzle fanatic. She would finish the crossword and the cryptogram from the *Hanniston Sentinel* before breakfast if she wasn't busy serving it up at Dora's Diner. Lately she'd been doing Sudoku puzzles, but only the five-star ones in the Sunday paper because the lower levels of difficulty were no challenge.

I remember taking every one of those magazines to Boley on visiting day. When the end of the month came around, he'd look through the plexiglass screen at me and say very seriously, "Don't you forget my crossword book next time, Dunne," like his life depended on it. All the time he had in his cell, I wondered why Boley did some puzzles to completion but never bothered with the others. I didn't wonder long, though. I opened the box and pulled out Baby.

I held the guitar flat across my lap and ran my hand down the neck. I plucked the double E string with my thumb and felt the deep vibration in my thighs. I rummaged in the prison envelope and pulled out one of Boley's copper picks. I tipped the guitar into playing position and fingered a chord. I dragged the copper pick across the strings and felt as if Boley finally had some closure to his life.

"Throw me a Kleenex."

Carlotta stared at me. "Are you tearing up?"

"No. There are fingerprints on the body from when somebody put Baby in the box."

Boley always wiped all his guitars down with a handkerchief, or his shirt tail when he was finished playing. He said with a laugh, "That way, I see fingerprints on the body, I know if anybody been playin' with it when I ain't around. Too bad I couldn't do that with my women."

I wiped Baby down and carefully laid her in the box. "I'm going down to Malone's. I want Johnny to see this."

Malone's Music is tucked between a deli and a hardware store on 7th Avenue, one of a long line of storefronts from a more prosperous era before malls and Internet shopping. The owners of these places are die-hards, some of them third generation, and they aren't giving up their piece of the American dream easily. Sometimes, though, as they lay off staff and cut their take-home pay to stay in business, they seem like old pugs trading off pounds, fighting out of their weight class to stay in the game.

Malone's isn't a flashy supermarket like Guitar Center or Sam Ash. The building is old, a dry goods store in the 30s. The sign out front is unpretentious and the merchandise behind the bars on the front window is carefully arranged to keep instruments and other gear out of the sun and out of the immediate reach of smash-and-grabbers from the sidewalk. Inside, the store is two floors and a basement filled with enough gear to outfit a dozen bands.

Johnny Malone and I had been friends since high school when we started playing together in garage bands, and he was one of the few people I could trust without reservation. I stamped the snow off my shoes and stepped inside. Malone's was my candy store. I can look at guitars in catalogs or magazine ads, or look at pictures of them on the Internet, but it never gives me the same kick as seeing them live in 3-D and thinking about what it would be like to play one of them. Old Strats, vintage Les Pauls, or an old Gretsch Country Gentleman. Johnny had them all, restored by his hand to perfection. Once in a while, I'd take one down, plug it into an amp and play, but most of the time, I just relished the thought. Like John Irving once wrote, "imagining something is always better than remembering something."

It was too early in the day for the heavy metal virtuosos who wandered in after school to play a chainsaw concerto on the demo equipment. Behind the counter, Johnny's clerk Nick was air-guitaring his way through Deep Purple's "Highway Star" as it played through one of those little blue tooth speakers that sound like a Wurlitzer jukebox. If you put a guitar in those empty hands, Nick wouldn't miss a note.

Times have changed. When I was a kid there were three basic choices: the Carcassi Classical Guitar Method, Nick Manoloff's guitar instruction books, and a brand new series by some guy named Mel Bay. If you wanted to play rock'n'roll, you wore out a 45 record and your parents' patience listening to it over and over to learn the chords, the lyrics, and especially the signature guitar riffs and solos. Nick's generation has all the resources: YouTube videos, Instruction DVDs, tablature on the Internet, and artist specific books to teach you how to play songs but not how to play music.

At different times when I taught guitar students, I insisted they learn to read standard musical notation, and I lost some students because of it. They'd come in and say, "Show me how to play that riff in (fill in the blank with your favorite guitar hero)." More than once I'd say, "okay," and write the riff out in standard notation on a piece of staff paper and let them figure out the odd fingerings and techniques that gave expression to it. Tablature is useful. Somebody spent weeks figuring out how to play a movement in a unique way or in the most economical fashion, and I can see at a glance how something was played on a recording, but it's not music. I always lean on a *Guitar Player* editorial I saw thirty years ago about reading music that said, "I've never seen a Fake Book of 500 Jazz Standards written in Tab." Amen.

"Sam the Man," Nick said. He's a tall, gangly guy with thick dark curls hanging out of his cap. Today, despite the snowy weather, he was wearing a wife-beater tank top over his jeans.

"Aren't you cold in that shirt?"

He laughed. "After all the pain to get the tats, man, you don't cover 'em up." Nick's arms were crawling with snakes and skulls and skeletal Goth women. "What's in the box? Don't tell me you're selling off and getting out."

"Cold day in hell. Nick. Where's Johnny?"

"Back in the Inner Sanctum." He jerked his thumb to the rear of the store, Johnny's workroom where he did all his repairs and restorations.

I carried Baby under my arm to the back of the main floor past Johnny's wall of guitars and amps and knocked on a door with a sign that read Employees Only. "Come on in, Sam." Johnny had a window installed over his workbench so that he could see the sales floor. "I trust Nick, and he's pretty sharp, but he can't see everything," Johnny told me once."

The door swung open, and the smell of glue, and lacquer mingled with the sweet scent of fine old wood; not the quick-dried stuff some guitar makers put into the instruments today, aged wood. "Hey Sam. Come on in."

I stepped into Johnny's workshop, a space the width of the store and about twenty feet deep. Unlike so many workshops, Johnny's was immaculate. Most people I knew littered the workbench with tools and parts and waited 'til the sawdust and detritus on the floor hit the six-inch mark before sweeping it out. Johnny's workshop was cleaner than most restaurant kitchens I've seen.

Johnny Malone stands half a head shorter than I do but he makes up for it in his shoulders. He's three-quarters bald, but refuses to yield to fashion and shave his head. That day he wore a shop apron with a red lacquer stain like a Rorschach blot across the bottom.

I set the box on the table beside a guitar neck in a straightening jig that looked like a chunk of a Roman aqueduct strapped to it with thick rubber tubing. The logo on the headstock under the carved M read "Mosrite". Under the brand I saw "The Ventures."

"Wow. I haven't seen one of these since the B-52s. Did you buy it?"

He shook his head. "No, I'm restoring it for the owner. They put a poor truss mechanism in the first five hundred or so, and his broke. I'm going to straighten the neck and try to pull out the old rod and replace it without doing too much cosmetic damage. He said he wants it to play good first, look good second. Look here." Johnny pointed to the serial number at the butt of the fingerboard: 0419.

"That ought to be worth a lot of money."

He nodded. "Yeah, Japanese collectors were paying as much as ten grand for one in just about any shape at one time. The Ventures faded away stateside, but in Japan, they're still gods. So what's in the box?"

"You won't believe it." I opened the box and took out Baby.

"Holy shit."

I had told Johnny about Baby and showed him the pictures I took when I got to play with Boley, but nothing prepared him for the reality of holding the guitar in his lap and wrapping his hand around the oversized neck. He fretted a barre chord and said, "I can feel my hands cramping up already. Were his fingers really that big?"

"I'm afraid so. Plug it into an amp. You have to hear how it sounds."

"I feel like that guy in *The Incredible Shrinking Man* when the whole world seems to be getting bigger. I feel like a six-year-old holding a Les Paul."

I had to admit I felt pretty much the same way the first time I held the guitar. Johnny handed Baby to me and dragged over an old Fender Twin he kept in the shop as a test amp. He plugged Baby in, and as soon as he did, the amp buzzed like a chainsaw.

"I don't get it," I said. "It never did that before. Could it be the amp?"

Johnny shook his head. "I just used it a half hour before you got here. Clean sound." He reached behind the amp and toggled the ground switch. No change. "Something must be shorting out in the wiring. Maybe a bad solder job, or something's touching the pickguard." He reached for a screwdriver from the peg board over the bench. "Shut off the amp. I'll take off the guard and troubleshoot the wiring."

Johnny plucked a Phillips screwdriver from a tool carousel and began removing screws. "What did he use that scarred this up so badly?"

"Copper picks as thick as a dime. What's the fancy musical term? Attack?" I laughed. "I think Boley took the word literally."

"One more screw." Johnny removed the last one and lifted the aluminum pickguard away. He laid it face down on the bench and moved his goose-necked lamp to shine into the cavity. "I think I see the problem. Look at that."

But I wasn't looking where Johnny was pointing. I was looking at the underside of the pickguard where someone had all but sanded away columns of numbers.

"Johnny, could you do something for me?"

"Sure, Sam, what's that?" He looked up from the guitar's multicolored entrails.

"Make me a pickguard just like this one and put it on the guitar. I'm taking this with me."

"I can do that. I'll have to get a piece of aluminum stock. But I have to ask why."

I turned the pickguard over and showed Johnny a handful of faint numbers blending into the swirling lines where someone had tried to rub them out and didn't quite finish the job. "I think Boley Watts was hedging against his memory and changed his mind."

Johnny traced the pickguard on a sheet of paper, marked the screw holes, and handed it to me. "The wiring fix is easy enough, but you'll have to leave the guitar here for a day if you want me to replace the guard."

"Let's keep this between ourselves for now, Johnny."

"What do you think the letters and numbers mean? Some kind of code?"

"I don't know, but I plan on finding out."

After supper, I sat for more than an hour at my desk in the living room studying the pickguard and trying to make out the numbers and letters that had been hand stamped into the aluminum with a hammer and dies then partially obliterated as if someone interrupted Boley before he could finish the job. A few letters and numbers on the outside edges of the group were legible, but the rest were lost.

"They look random," Carlotta said over my shoulder. "That's the best kind of code. If it was simple letter substitution, it would be simple enough. There are even computer apps you can download to crack those, though that takes the fun out of solving them. It's tough to solve something like this unless you have a key."

"If there's a key, Boley took it with him."

"It's the missing money, isn't it?"

I hadn't said it out loud; afraid of what evil gods might be listening and give the idea legs, but Carlotta gave voice to what I was thinking. "Yeah, that is a good bet."

"It would be a lot easier if we had the whole set of numbers."

"There may be a way to make that happen." I stood up and pulled my bomber jacket from the coat tree by the door. "I'm going to Roy's later. I need to talk to Razor."

Razor is a friend of mine; at least I'm the closest thing he has to a friend that I know of. Heavy metal guitarist from ten 'til two, and master thief in the wee hours. He bankrolls his band, Blood Lightning by the proceeds from his burglary. Razor may not be the most dangerous person I know, but he's in the top three. If anyone would know about obliterated numbers, he would. I had a phone number where I could reach him committed to memory, but Razor told me it was for emergencies only. "Don't call this number unless somebody's cutting your throat." But I knew where I could find him.

"Want to come along?"

Carlotta shook her head. "No, honey. Too rough for me. People there'd put a bullet in your head and throw you over in a corner for five bucks or just for laughs. If you go there, you'll need all your energy watching out for yourself. I'd just be a distraction."

XIII

There are days when I wish I never had a phone. I've felt that way most of my adult life, but cell phones up the ante. It was bad enough for decades to have the phone jangle right beside my head and yank me out of a deep sleep or interrupt even the most intimate moments, but at least that only happened at home. Now that I have a cell phone, people can call me day or night and expect me to answer by the third ring. If I let a call go to voice mail, I get a snarky message like, "Why do you even have a cell phone if you don't answer it," "If I wanted to leave a message, I'd've called your landline and talked to the answering machine," or my favorite, "You never listen to your messages anyway, so I'm not going to leave one."

I happened to be at home the morning after my meeting with Weintraub when the phone rang. Carlotta was out grocery shopping, so I was It. Caller ID told me the caller was from the 412 area code, a Pittsburgh number.

"Hello?"

"I'm calling for Samuel Dunne." That name again, Samuel. Nobody calling to hire me for a gig. I guess I waited too long to respond. "Is this Mr. Dunne?"

In spite of myself, I let irritation steer the car. "Yeah, this is Sam Dunne Who are you and what do you want?"

"My name is Charles Tanner, Mr. Dunne. Your name was given to me by Attorney Herbert Weintraub." The voice was smooth, almost practiced in its delivery. There was a trace of accent, maybe mid-western, Kansas or Nebraska, but was pretty well hidden. "I understand you were the sole beneficiary of Bolton Watts' will and that he left his guitar to you." In the back of my mind, an alarm bell went off. This was just too quick.

"And if that's true?"

"I represent a party who collects rare guitars, and he would be interested in buying it from you." Party. No name. That told me that either the collector was a money belt with a name I'd recognize and I'd jack up the price accordingly, or something shady was in the works. At this moment Carlotta walked in with two sacks of groceries.

"I hadn't even thought about selling the guitar. I may keep it for sentimental reasons." Carlotta frowned at my tone and craned her neck to see the number on the ID screen.

"I can assure you, Mr. Dunne—may I call you Sam?"

"No." I sounded like a prick, but Tanner's pushiness annoyed me.

"All right—Mr. Dunne. The guitar is unique, and my client wants it."

"I'm not ready to —"

He ignored me and went on. "Think it over, Mr. Dunne. I can assure you that my client will match any offer you may get and better it."

"Like I started to say, I'm not ready to make any commitments."

"Well please think it over, won't you? May I call you back in a day or two?"

"Don't expect me to answer the phone." I love Caller ID. I wish it was invented twenty years earlier than it was.

"Well, if you do decide, my number is," and he rattled off the same number that was showing on my phone.

"Don't hold your breath." I hung up.

Carlotta set the grocery bags on the coffee table. "What was that all about?"

"Some guy named Tanner who wants to buy Baby."

"Why were you so rude with him?"

"His attitude pissed me off. He sounded like it was all a done deal before I ever answered the phone."

"How much did he offer you?"

"We never got that far."

"It's your decision, Sam, keep it or sell it."

"Maybe I'll donate it to the Rock and Roll Hall of Fame."

"They've got enough guitars already." She picked up the grocery bags and started for the kitchen. She stopped and turned back. "What do you know about this Tanner?"

"Just his name. That and he's from Pittsburgh." I knew that from the area code. Years ago, to free up more available numbers for internet servers, the telephone company changed area codes around Pittsburgh. 412 became solely for the immediate Pittsburgh area, and the surrounding counties that previously shared the area code were reassigned other numbers. A friend of mine who lived South of Pittsburgh in a city called Connellsville complained that it cost him a bundle to change his letterhead, his advertising, and the info on the sides of his trucks. "The worst part of it all is the numerology," he said. "Our area code used to be 412; add the digits and get lucky number seven. Add up 724 and what do you get? Thirteen."

"Let's look him up online." Carlotta clicked the mouse and my desktop screen lit up. She sat down and clicked on Google. She typed in Charles Tanner, Pittsburgh, Pennsylvania, and the phone number. In a minute, she said, "Uh-oh."

There are three Charles Tanners in Pittsburgh, but only one with the magic phone number. The phone was listed to Charles W. Tanner, Private Detective.

XIV

It turned out that leaving Baby with Johnny Malone was my best idea of the week. Carlotta's days off were Tuesday and Wednesday, so she was home, busy vacuuming the living room, something I didn't do often enough. Someday she'll find the carpet under all the dust and grit. The sweeper was so loud I almost didn't hear the doorbell.

I said in her ear, "Somebody at the door." She shut off the vacuum and

"What was that all about?"

I peered out the peephole. Two men, tall, in raincoats, one hatless and one with a short-brimmed fedora. Cops.

"Yeah?" I said through the door.

"Mr. Dunne?"

"Yeah."

"FBI. Would you please open the door." Not a question, an imperative. At least he didn't say please with his foot.

They took a step back and I slipped off the burglar chain and opened the door. "May I see some ID?" I could be polite too, up to a point.

Both opened their foldovers. They were definitely Feebs, badges and all. Either of them was an inch or two taller than I, and very buff in that broad-shouldered, lean-hipped way they stamp them out at Quantico. The speaker, the guy in the hat was named Blankenship. His cohort had a name I'd never seen before. "T-A-J-C," I read from his folder. "Looks like an eye chart. How do you say that one?"

His mouth smiled, but his eyes didn't. He was the cold one of the pair. The smile was a mask. I got the feeling he could kill me without blinking if I made a wrong move, and that smile would never leave his face. "It's pronounced like 'touch' with a long I." He said it for me and I repeated it.

"That's a new one for me. What do you want?"

"We'd like to talk to you. May we come in?"

Instinct kicked in. I stepped into the hall and pulled the door shut behind me. Carlotta had been listening too. I heard her slip the chain and throw the deadbolt. Having a savvy woman like her watch my back is an absolute gift. "Got a warrant?"

"No," Blankenship said, "but all we want is—"

"There's your answer. Maybe you can badge your way past Jerry the super and get in the building, but if you want to come in my private residence, you'll need the paperwork."

Blankenship looked peeved, but Tajc's smile didn't change one iota. "We just have a few questions."

"Ask away. We can hear each other fine out here." Blankenship looked up and down the hallway.

"Oh, never mind the neighbors, the walls are so thin everybody knows everybody's business anyway."

"I don't understand your antagonism, Mr. Dunne." Blankenship stood stock still but Tajc shifted his feet, ready for a signal that never came. "Attorney Herbert Weintraub informed us that you were the sole beneficiary of Bolton Watts' will." Didn't have to look at his notes. This one was sharp. "We only want to ask you about the guitar he left you."

"You're the second person to ask about it this week."

The agents traded a look, and I knew I hit a live wire. "Who else contacted you?" This from Tajc. No Mr. Dunne this time.

I grinned. "Weintraub didn't mention that little detail? You're the FBI. I shouldn't have to tell you. Don't you have a tap on my phone already?" I could almost see steam coming from Blankenship's shirt collar. "Now, if you gentlemen will excuse me, I'm going to go back to pursuing my private, legal business."

I reached behind me and gave a three-tap on the door. I heard the chain slip and the lock click. "You gentlemen have a nice afternoon." The door opened behind me and I slipped back into the apartment before either agent could say another word.

I waited until I heard the ding of the elevator bell before I said anything. I noticed that the pickguard was no longer in sight on my desk. Carlotta had put it under a sofa cushion. "Thanks, darlin'. That was quick thinking."

"*De nada.* What's up with this?"

"I'm guessing the Bureau still has an open file on Boley's last bank job. He dies, they watch where his stuff goes, and they follow it looking for clues. They want the money. It's an embarrassment to the FBI that they never found it. They're hoping Boley's guitar will lead them to the stash."

"So what are you going to do?"

"Keep Baby away from them."

"I know this won't win me any points, but why don't you cooperate?"

"Because they're cops. Fancy cops, but they're cops. When Boley was arrested, they beat him nearly to death and he wouldn't give it up. I'd feel like I betrayed him if I so much as greased the wheels for those bastards."

"Oh, Sam." Carlotta sighed and shook her head. She took my face in her hands and looked me in the eyes. "I just hope they don't do the same to you before this is over."

"I'll second that." By the look of Tajc, I figured my turn would be as bad as Boley's or worse.

XV

Hanniston always looked better the first hour of a snow storm before the pristine white turned to slush gray in the streets. Snow covers a multitude of sins, litter, and crud, and when the sky clears and that bright afternoon sun breaks through the clouds, the city almost looks reborn. Almost.

I'd given the FBI boys an hour to get bored waiting for me to pop out and lead them to who or what they were after. I called the time and weather service and Dial-a-Prayer on the landline in case they were listening in and then put on my bomber jacket. I purposely went to two bars for one beer each and walked out the back door of both in case I was being tailed. Then when I was sure I was clear, I went to Roy's.

Roy's is a bar with pool tables in the front and card tables in the back, plus an occasional craps game in the corner. No drugs allowed, but just about every other criminal element frequents the place. I figured I'd find Razor there as likely as anywhere else.

I opened the door and a blast of hot air laced with smoke steamrolled out, accompanied by a roaring jukebox. I've never seen anybody put a quarter in the juke at Roy's or ever punch in a number. The old Rock-Ola just blasts away from opening 'til closing as a courtesy to the patrons; it makes audio surveillance all but impossible. A heavy-set bald guy in a Tap Out sweatshirt sat just inside at a small table like a desk. A baseball bat leaned against the table, and a .38 lay ready in a drawer. Pony's job was checking IDs, not for age but for police affiliation. Cops and stoolies weren't welcome in Roy's. He had an unfiltered Camel in the corner of his mouth burned down close enough to catch his bushy moustache on fire if he moved the wrong way.

"How's it going, Sam?" he said around the cigarette.

"You know, Pony. Comes and goes."

"Mostly goes for me." He laughed at his own joke.

"I hear you. Busy tonight?"

He nodded and the neon Michelob sign beside him flashed on his bare scalp. "Cold weather brings them all in off the street."

"Me too." It is a mark of status that I'm known and welcomed in Roy's, largely because of Razor, but I wouldn't put it on my resume.

I scanned the bar and didn't see Razor at first. I strolled around the L and saw him sitting in a booth with a woman. It was obviously business. She wasn't his date, or she'd sitting on his side instead of across the table.

The woman looked to be in her mid-fifties, with hair dyed like India ink and a leathery carny suntan that made her look like she ate broken glass for breakfast and chased it with Drano. Standing just behind her, back to the booth, was a man in a cashmere topcoat and a furred hat like you see in old cold war movies set in the Kremlin. His piggy eyes roamed the room, looking at everything and everybody except her. His left hand never left his coat pocket.

Without even turning his head, Razor acknowledged me with a "one-minute" gesture. I sat on a stool and ordered a draft, paid with a five, and left the change on the bar. Sometimes Razor's one minute turned into an hour, and Roy's wouldn't run a tab for the Pope. In the mirror I watched as Razor and his table mate talked back and forth, she gesturing continuously as she spoke, and Razor sitting, hands flat on the table, neither his face nor his eyes giving anything away. Two beers later, the negotiations were done. The woman stood, nodded at Razor, and she and her human pit bull stalked out of Roy's.

I turned on the stool and saw Razor wave me over and I picked up my beer and left the change for the bartender. I slid into the booth as Razor held up two fingers. The bartender nodded and moved down the bar to run two more drafts.

On stage, Razor looks every inch the heavy metal bad boy; lean and sinuous as a cobra, he stalks the stage holding his guitar less like a musical instrument than a weapon spewing cascades of shrieking notes like a terrorist with an Uzi, his lank hair and drops of sweat flying as he whips his head back and forth. He never takes a drug, but you'd bet he was shot up with meth as he struts nonstop across the stage, fingers flying up and down the fretboard and slicing ears off the first ten rows.

Tonight, he wore a blue and gold sweatshirt with the logo for the Hanniston Wildcats, the local minor league baseball team, and a black toboggan with his hair tucked underneath. His usual three-day growth of blond beard was missing. Must have been an important meeting, I thought. He went formal.

"Who's the gypsy woman?" I said.

"Somebody you're better off not knowing about. So, Sam, what's up? Must be important to drag you out in the cold."

"You won't believe it." I told him about inheriting Boley Watts' guitar, my trip to Weintraub's office, my phone call from Tanner, and my visit from Blankenship and Tajc. His eyes widened a little when I mentioned the missing bank money. A hundred grand is a great attention getter.

"You did the right thing with the Feebs. If they come back with a warrant, they're legit for sure. If they don't, watch your ass. They may be working their own agenda. Old case everybody forgot about; find the money and don't tell. Who's to know?" He put a Lucky Strike in the corner of his mouth. Razor's a traditionalist; he still smokes unfiltered Luckies, although he has to get them from Kentucky. I smoked them myself before I quit cold. I liked the taste of the tobacco, and I could leave a pack of Luckies on the bar, go play a set with the band, and come back to find them untouched. It's been twenty years since I've smoked a cigarette, but there are still days when I'm nervous or angry that I feel like lighting one up.

Razor turned the open pack toward me. "Go ahead, Sam. You know you want one." It was a standing joke between us.

I laughed. "Get thee behind me, Razor. I'll keep my lungs, thanks."

His face got serious. "So, what do you need me to do?"

"Tomorrow, I need you to go to Malone's and get Baby out of there. Too many people are interested in it for my peace of mind. If I go myself, the agents might follow me and get their hands on it. I'll call Johnny to let him know, and you can pick it up tomorrow whenever you're ready."

"Why not just call him now? I can meet him at the store."

"The store's closed by now. I'll have to call him at home. I don't want anything to look out of the ordinary. I want them to think Baby's still in my apartment. If they see my 'known acquaintances' shuffling around after hours, they might tumble to what's happening. Just keep it safe for me."

Razor nodded. "Will do. A hundred twenty grand, huh?"

"Give or take." I told him about the sequential bills, and he never blinked. I figured Razor had the connections to launder the money if he got his hands on it. "One more thing. What do you know about restoring engraved serial numbers?" I quickly explained the embossed columns on the pickguard.

Razor stubbed out his cigarette on his beer coaster. "I know a guy. I'll make a call and get back to you."

XVI

Walking out of Roy's and stepping into the February cold was like pulling my head out my armpit for a breath of air. I called Johnny from a pay phone. I understand why crooks buy burner cell phones. Takes a while to find a pay phone these days. They've become an endangered species. Johnny answered at home and I explained what I wanted him and Razor to do.

"Got it. I'll have the guitar ready. I'll put it in a Gibson or Yamaha box if I can find one that fits. While it was apart, I poked around the inside. No notes or papers or any other surprises stashed in the cavities. By the way, Sam, I fixed the buzz; she plays like Gabriel's trumpet now."

"That's great. Did you replace the pickguard?"

"Yeah. I made a new one just like the original. I even dug pick marks in it so it looks authentic."

"Thanks, Johnny." I hung up the phone and hoped that I hadn't dragged my friends into anything that would hurt them or worse. Newspaper woman Wendy Conn once accused me of "dancing on the edge" as she put it, taking chances with my life and anybody else's who happens to be around. I guess it's a fair cop, but I try to not think about it much. Most of the time it doesn't matter anyway. I always disliked the saying, "It is what it is"; sometimes it fits the occasion, but I try to never pull somebody's eyes shut into a situation.

My biggest worry in all this was Carlotta. She was tough and saved my ass on one occasion, but I had the feeling that I was dealing with some world-class bad people this time, and I didn't want to see her caught in the middle.

Then there was the money. What if we found it? Did Boley even want it found? He etched the code on the pickguard then scratched it off as an afterthought. Or did he erase most of it and leave enough to put me onto where he hid the money? Or was it a lead to the money at all? Thinking about it gave me a headache, or maybe it was all the beer I drank.

When I got home, the apartment was full of the smell of pan-fried scallops and black-eyed peas. Carlotta was no gourmet chef, but she never cooked me a meal I didn't enjoy. She was standing at the stove, and I wrapped my arms around her from behind then I pulled down the neck of her T-shirt and kissed the Virgo symbol tattooed on her left shoulder. I started sliding a hand under her shirt and she said, "One thing at a time, Sam. The scallops will be ready in two minutes. I'll be ready all night."

"Okay, boss," I said, laughing. I started for the fridge for a Heineken, and changed my mind. One more beer might crash the rest of the evening. Pushing fifty has its hazards.

The scallops were great, and Carlotta was greater. Afterward, we lay under the covers. She had a habit of cuddling up to me with a leg thrown over mine, a habit I didn't discourage since it sometimes led to round two.

As I often did, I reached around her and played air guitar, singing Mississippi John Hurt's "Big Leg Blues":

Raise up, baby, get your big leg offa mine
Raise up, baby, get your big leg offa mine
They're so heavy, make a good man change his mind

She turned her head and bit my shoulder.

"Ow."

"Is that how you see me? Heavy?" she said with mock indignation. "You can cook your own scallops next time."

"Naah, 'you ain't heavy,' I sang in Bee Gees manque, 'you're my woman.' I wouldn't even say Reubenesque or stout. Substantial, that's the word." She is, admittedly, a little thick in the middle, but it suited her, gave her a certain Earth Mother allure. "Substantially sexy and lusciously lascivious. That's what I say."

She laughed. "That's what I get for hooking up with an English prof songwriter, a line of bullshit a mile long and a vocabulary to match."

"And look what I've got: a crossword puzzle fanatic with one that puts mine to shame."

She propped herself on one elbow and let her breasts lie on my chest. "Ain't it great?"

My hand crept over. "The best."

The nicest thing about round two is nobody rings the bell to stop.

XVII

The next morning, Carlotta needed milk for her signature blueberry pancakes. As I walked three blocks to the Mini Mart, I heard a blaring horn behind me. I turned around in time to see a beat-up white Buick Century creeping along at about five miles an hour with an impatient trucker behind it. There were two black guys in the front seat, and when they saw me looking at them, the driver cracked the gas and the car sped away. They didn't look like FBI agents, so I thought maybe they were sub-contracting with Tanner to follow me. I didn't have a chance to get the whole license number, but it was definitely a Pennsylvania plate, and I caught the last two numbers: 32.

I decided I would have to buy one of those Chiclet-sized cyclist mirrors to clip on my sunglasses to give me eyes behind. The situation was slipping past annoyance to serious concern.

As I stood at the checkout counter with the milk and a newspaper with puzzles for Carlotta, my eye drifted over the clerk's shoulder to the cigarette rack. I didn't give in, but the temptation was getting some traction. I looked both ways when I stepped out the door onto the sidewalk. No white Buick. Maybe they were just looking for an address, I thought. But my gut knew better.

Outside my building, I saw a nondescript green Chevy four-door parked up the block. If cops want an unmarked car to pass scrutiny, they have to learn to buy them with full wheel covers instead of those little chrome ashtray hub caps that leave half the wheel naked. The engine was running; I could see a cloud of exhaust pluming behind the car. I could also see two figures in the front seat. My tax dollars at work. Maybe Blankenship and Tajc got their warrant and they were waiting to make sure I was home before trying to serve it. I waved. Nobody waved back and nobody got out of the car.

I fished out my key and went inside. In the foyer, I stopped to get the mail and when I unlocked my box, an envelope with no stamp fluttered out. In it was an ad for a Monster Truck Show that night at the local arena. That was Razor's m.o. The ad was wrapped around a ticket in the cheap seats at the top tier. I've always hoped that someday Razor would pick something like a symphony concert or a Shakespeare production to meet, but I know that noise cover is a priority consideration.

I told Carlotta about the ticket, and she said, "So you're going to the redneck ballet, huh?"

"Yeah. Razor's taking me to meet with some guy who might be able to restore the numbers on the pickguard."

I had seen a few cop shows and read a few detective novels in which serial numbers filed off an engine block or a stolen pistol were restored using some hell broth of chemicals, and I hoped Razor's friend could do the job with the pickguard. The thought crossed my mind to research the process on the Internet, but I remembered what slimy tentacles the cops and the FBI had. Homeland Security's made Internet privacy a hazy area these days. I figured they weren't above subpoenaing my browser records, or just hacking into my wi-fi and watching over my shoulder. Instant information is a great convenience, but as Barry Commoner's First Law of Ecology says, "Everything is connected to everything," and his Fourth

Law of Ecology says, "There is no such thing as a free lunch." Sometimes, patience does serve.

XVIII

Carlotta dropped me off at the Hanniston Arena a half hour before the Monster Truck Fest was scheduled to start. Based on the lines at all six ticket windows, you'd've thought Elvis and Johnny Cash came back for one night only. As I walked through the entrance, I saw a crowd huddled in a roped-off area outside one of the exit doors having one last cigarette before the show. The day after Pennsylvania passed a general smoking ban in public places, the Arena set aside one place for ticket holders to step out and have a smoke. You've never seen such a gang of miserable, pissed-off people as hockey fans in the sub-zero dead of winter, trying to connect a match flame with the end of a cigarette while they shiver from the cold during half-time. The new lepers. I feel their pain.

I noticed a number of the people waiting in line had shooter's earmuffs pulled down around their necks. That was a clue as to why vendors were selling souvenir programs for three dollars and earplugs for five. I didn't bother with the program, but I figured ten thousand rednecks can't be wrong. I bought the earplugs.

The promoters had converted the Arena, home to Hanniston Bobcat hockey games, basketball tournaments, and mid-level rock concerts into the world's biggest sandbox. The Monster Truck promoters had imported a couple thousand cubic yards of dirt and buried the arena floor under a six-foot-thick layer of native clay. Deep enough for a grave, I thought, though people usually didn't die at these things, but when they did, it wasn't usually the drivers of these stentorian monstrosities. The victims are more often people in the first six rows or once in a while a crewman, and once even a promoter. I was glad to be in the nosebleed seats, which, by the way, were packed. Razor's seat was the only one empty in the section.

The dirt on the floor was sculpted into mounds and ramps to facilitate the four-wheeling acrobatics of the monster trucks with names like Killcar, The Pulverizer, and Ramzilla. Dead center I saw two pairs of ramps that bookended a line of vans painted with stars and stripes ripe for crushing under the tractor-tired monsters. A girl, whose name was drowned out by the hooting of the crowd, came out in a fringed bikini top, red hot pants, a ten-gallon hat, and tooled cowboy boots to sing a painful rendition of the Star Spangled Banner.

In seconds, the arena filled with a roar that literally hurt my ears and justified the five-dollar earplugs. The trucks came blazing out of the entrance at the far end as the hillbilly nightingale ran for cover. The brightly painted trucks, some with energy drink or auto parts logos on their doors, roofs, and hoods rode twelve feet tall on chevroned tires. Unmuffled exhausts roared like dinosaurs through their hoods, a chromed pipe for each cylinder.

The jacked-up independent suspensions made the trucks look like weird insects and allowed them to twist and turn like triple-jointed circus freaks. The drivers cut donuts, popped wheelies, flew through the air off the ramps, tipped sideways to run on two wheels, and generally performed stunts I'd associate with BMX bikers and hardcore skaters. I've always believed that a whole generation of kids learned to drive by watching *The Dukes of Hazard*. They found a home in monster trucking.

Razor dropped into the seat next to me as a truck painted in a Stars and Bars motif combined a wheelie and a ramp run to go up on one wheel. It went fifty feet in that attitude then bounced back to earth. I hoped the driver was wearing a mouthpiece, otherwise, he'd be picking up his teeth from the floor of the cab. The crowd was cheering, but the sound was crushed by the bellow of the Dixie Cruiser's exhaust. Through some trick or another, an impressive burst of flame shot out of the pipes like dragon's breath.

Razor was wearing a forest green parka that I recognized from the Land's End catalog, its hood strategically arranged around his face. He made a motion for me to come with him, and we picked our way over a row of Tony Lamas and Red Wings to the aisle and the exit. In the corridor, the noise was marginally less deafening. Razor said something I couldn't hear, so I pulled out one of the earplugs as he repeated himself. "Hang this on your jacket." He handed me what I recognized from my years as a rocker to be a backstage all-access pass. He clipped one to the pocket of his coat and motioned for me to follow him.

Even with earplugs, the noise on the floor seemed worse than it was in the rafters, if that's possible. We walked around the floor, staying behind the wall of hay bales that ringed the action. Razor seemed perfectly at home, but I kept waiting for the fanged snout of Truckula to come bounding over the bales and swallow me. We got to the passageway at the far end just as a truck named the Damyankee, the monster truck equivalent of a pro wrestling villain, was revving its engine to make a grand entrance. I followed Razor as he turned a corner and flashed his badge at a security guard who unlocked a door leading to the locker room area. The door closed behind us, and like magic, the roar of the show dropped by half.

I took the earplugs out in time to hear Razor to say, "Barnum was right." We passed through the locker room and he led the way down a corridor to a door marked No Entry. It was unlocked and opened into a stairwell that led to the bowels of the building. At the bottom of the stairs we found a door marked Maintenance. Razor knocked and we stepped inside.

The windowless room was a workroom and storage area twice the size of my apartment. The Zamboni was parked in a far corner, and bales of paper towels and toilet paper were stacked eight high. The place smelled of disinfectant and motor oil. A bearded man in workman's coveralls and a grease-stained cap stood just inside. He nodded to Razor and eyed me up and down, more from curiosity than anything else.

Razor turned to me. "Give Snick the piece."

I handed over the pickguard and Snick seemed surprised. Maybe when Razor said "piece," Snick thought Razor meant a pistol. He turned it over in his hands, looking at it from every angle. "Aluminum. Should be simple enough." His voice was ragged, as if he'd had a throat injury at some point in his life. We followed him back to a cluttered workbench where he swept a pile of odds and ends aside with his forearm and swung a work light over to shine directly on the job.

He set a small metal toolbox on the bench and took out a jar the size of a 45-record spindle and one of those one-time throwaway brushes techs use for caustic chemicals. Then he pulled out a nine-volt battery with a foot long wire ending in an alligator clip soldered onto the positive terminal and a wire with a bare end attached to the negative. He swung a magnifying lens over and studied the scratches in the metal. "Looks as if he used a wire wheel. Didn't really cut too deep. I'll see what I can do." Snick took a sheet of emery cloth from the toolbox. "Make yourselves comfy. This'll take a few minutes." He started working the red cloth back and forth, methodically polishing the defacing marks out of the metal. He switched to fine steel wool a few minutes later and soon, the underside of the pickguard shone to an almost mirror polish.

Snick pulled a pair of safety goggles from a pigeonhole above the bench and pulled on rubber gloves. "Step back," he rasped. "You don't want any of this to get on you, and the fumes won't do you much good either." He clamped the alligator clip onto the aluminum and wrapped the bare end of the other wire around a ball of cotton.

"Stamping compresses the metal and etching takes away the less dense material from the surface and leaves the denser stuff if you don't etch off too much. Get a pencil and paper ready. I can't guarantee what will show or how long it will last."

I pulled a small spiral notebook and a ballpoint pen out of my jacket. Snick opened the jar and dipped a glass rod into it. He wiped the etching solution onto the cotton and began to gently spread it with light careful strokes across the polished surface. "The electric current helps things along a little," Snick said. "Gotta be careful now." He stopped the application, turned the metal to study it at an angle, then set it down. "Not yet." He gave it five strokes and checked again. Five more. "Got something. You ready?"

He read off the numbers slowly, deliberately, row by row as Sam jotted them down. When he finished, Sam had six rows of six numbers each in a block of thirty-six digits.

When he was finished, Snick unclipped the battery and said, "Now what? You want the marks gone forever, or do you want the whole piece destroyed? Either way's no problem."

Razor looked to me. "Your call, Sam."

I thought it over. The safest way was to destroy the pickguard completely, but a part of me wanted to keep Baby all original. "Wipe it clean."

"Will do." Snick turned on a bench grinder and in less than a minute the code was gone forever.

"Take it with you," I said to Razor, and he slipped it into his jacket. He fanned a pair of hundred-dollar bills and handed them to Snick, who nodded and rasped, "Always a pleasure."

In five minutes, I was going out one service exit and Razor was going out another. In my pocket was a set of letters and numbers that might lead to Boley's missing money. All I had to do was figure out what they meant.

Back at the apartment, I sat at my desk with a beer and Carlotta and I kicked around the possibilities for the code. We tried letters for numbers; A is 1, B is 2, and so forth. We ran the system from left to right and right to left, starting with the upper left corner and the lower right. All we got was gibberish. By then it was midnight. Carlotta had to be up for work at five, so we called it a night. I lay in bed staring up at the ceiling, the numbers running through my head nonstop. What do the numbers mean, Boley? What do they mean?

"Step back," he rasped.

XIX

Carlotta was at work, and I was sitting at my desk sorting out receipts for my income tax. No matter how good my intentions are, I always end up filing on April 15 because making a piecemeal living is so detailed and I have so many interruptions. Like the phone. The landline rang, and the number was one I didn't recognize. I was going to let it go to voice mail, but it just was too annoying. I picked it up and said, "Hello?"

Silence, then a hang-up. I wrote the number on a notepad in case they called back. I went back to work and in five minutes, someone knocked at the door. That was the second time in three days that someone came up without ringing the bell downstairs in the lobby. I was tempted to take my pistol out of the drawer in my desk but decided that if it was the FBI, things could go south in a hurry, even though I have a carry permit.

I looked out the peephole and saw a man in a belted olive-green raincoat and a respectable hat. He stared at the peephole as if he could see me looking at him, and smiled. I realized that my shadow showed on the tiny lens outside. He knocked again.

I opened the door a little and left the burglar chain intact. I looked out and saw that the guy in the raincoat was still smiling. "Good morning, Mr. Dunne. My name is Charles Tanner. We spoke on the telephone."

I already decided I didn't like him from our previous conversation. The used-car salesman smile wasn't helping his case. "How did you get into the building?"

He ignored my question. Tanner was about my height, and the raincoat cinched at the middle accentuated a trim waist. I looked at the knuckles of his left hand, the one holding the briefcase, and saw a variety of scars where he'd split them on people's teeth. A few more scars over his eyebrows told me he was a boxer once, maybe a welterweight who never went pro but decided to become a leg breaker instead.

"I just dropped by to see whether you'd decided to sell the guitar, maybe let me take a photo of it to text to my client." The voice in person was as polished as it had been on the phone, though I didn't doubt Tanner could shift into tough guy mode like snapping his fingers.

"Why does this mysterious anonymous collector you represent need a private eye to do his leg work for him?"

Tanner blinked. I'd caught him off guard, like somebody in the ring who feinted then nailed him with a punch he didn't see coming. He recovered quickly and made a dismissive "you got me" gesture with his free hand. "Sometimes, Mr. Dunne, people are difficult to locate."

"You mean like Boley Watts? Seems to me he was at the same address for twenty-two years and as far as I knew, he didn't plan to move. And I'm in the phone book. Try again, pal."

No response.

"All I can say is you're stupid if you think I am. Tell your client if I decide to sell, it will be to anybody but him." I started to close the door.

"Can't we talk about this? I can guarantee that the price will be far more than you make in a year playing one-nighters and teaching English Comp at the community college."

"You left out recording royalties."

"Won't you reconsider?"

I thought about it for a second, then said something I probably shouldn't have. "Yeah. Tell your mysterious client I'll sell him the guitar—for 120 grand in cash in non-sequential bills and two plane tickets to Rio."

That comment knocked down all the pins. This time, Tanner didn't recover so easily. The smile froze on his face, but his eyes gave him away. I decided I'd like to play Texas Hold 'em with him sometime. I was sure I could send him home in his BVDs.

"Look, Mr. Dunne," he started.

"Go away." I shut the door and ended the conversation. A minute later, I looked out the peephole and he was still standing there, maybe pondering what to do next. A minute after that, I looked out again, and he was gone, but I knew that wasn't the last I'd see of him.

A little later, the phone rang. It was Joe Mancini, my agent. "Sam? You're gonna love this. I just got off the phone with Brian Halpern. I've got you a week in Jensen Beach, Florida."

"When? July or August?" Joe was always getting me gigs in the off-season, never in prime time.

"Next week, three-nighter at Roland's."

"What's Roland's?"

"Beach front restaurant. You'll play eight to eleven Friday through Sunday at the bar."

"Not bad. How'd that happen?"

"The word is that the guy who was supposed to do the gig got sick."

"How do you plan an illness a week in advance? It's like planning to break your leg. Sounds like 'green flu' to me."

Mancini laughed. "Nothing makes you sicker than an offer of mo' money."

"That's for sure."

"And there's more. As a bonus I have you slotted to sing the National Anthem for one of the Mets' spring training games at First Data Field."

"Where's that?"

"Down the road in Port St. Lucie."

"That's great, Joe. Carlotta'll love it."

"So, you're in?"

"I'm in."

"Great. I'll fax the contract to you along with all the details."

"Thanks, Joe." I hung up feeling pretty good for the first time in a while, but it didn't last.

That night, I was slated to play at Casey's, a restaurant and bar on Hanniston's North Side. It's a friendly gig, nice crowd, and lots of people between thirty-five and fifty who want to hang out somewhere they don't have to listen to Hip-Hop blaring from some DJ's system and get thrown into a seizure by the flashing light show. I've been playing there regularly for a couple of years, and I keep a spare set of gear in a closet next to the six-by-eight platform that passes for a stage.

Carlotta goes with me most times, it's her "night out" as she calls it, and I'm always glad to see her out in the crowd. Tonight, we talked about it. "Maybe you should sit this one out, darlin'," I said. "I've got people following me, and I don't know what they might do."

"Then maybe I should go to watch your back."

"I've always done best in a bad situation when I don't have anyone but myself to protect. No offense, C, but you'd be a distraction and I'd hate to see either of us get hurt, especially you."

She pouted, but I knew it wasn't genuine. She knew I was right. "Okay, Sam, but if you come home with lipstick on your shirt, I'll wash it out with your blood."

I saluted. "Yes, Ma'am." Then she laughed and kissed me. I've lost count how many times I've been glad we found each other.

The job ran from nine 'til midnight, early hours for the bar trade. For almost twenty years, I played in bands that hauled two truckloads of equipment, took two hours to set up, played from ten 'til two, took another hour to tear down and load up, then drove an hour to get home just in time for the sunrise. When I developed a solo act, I went from two truckloads of gear to a guitar, an amp, a stool, and a microphone; set up in ten minutes, tear down in five, early hours, and a quiet repertoire. What's not to like?

People laugh when I refer to "going to work." They say, "That's not work." If it isn't, why do people pay me to do it? Some nights, my job isn't to play guitar and sing, it's to keep drunken adults amused so they don't punch each other or break the furniture. Casey's is nothing like that. It's a corner building in old-style Sullivanesque architecture that offers three floors. The bar is on the ground level for walk-in business, the second floor has tables for restaurant customers, and the third is an event room for meetings, receptions, and parties.

The bar area seats sixty people, give or take. It has a high stamped tin ceiling that makes for tricky acoustics, but years of playing there have taught me how to handle my sound. The bar itself is a beauty; twenty-five feet, give or take, of polished mahogany with brass foot rails, original equipment from the thirties. The light comes from an array of neon beer signs that cast a colorful glow all over the room.

Mark, the owner is a musician's friend. He always keeps an eye on the crowd. Nobody hassles or heckles the talent for more than a minute before he stops it. Mark is about three inches taller than I and built like a linebacker, which he was in college. He's as affable a person as you'd want to meet unless somebody causes trouble in his place. I've seen him haul two people out bodily by their shirts, one in each hand. I'm glad he's on my side. Tonight, he was wearing a crew-necked sweater that changed color every time he passed a different beer sign.

He walked by carrying two cases of Bud Light as I was setting up my gear. "How's it going, Sam?"

"*Mezza mezza*, Mark. You?"

"Business has been slow this month, people paying off Christmas bills and staying home in the bad weather, but I'm still making the nut."

"That's good news. I'd hate to see you close. Where would I work?"

"I hear the Home for the Deaf is hiring. Where's herself?"

"Taking the night off. Even she gets tired of listening to me once in a while."

Mark laughed. "Knock 'em dead, Sam."

I angle the spots on the stage so they don't shine straight into my eyes.

I like to keep eye contact with the crowd, gauge their response to what I'm playing, and know when it's time to shift gears. Tonight the crowd looked like a lot of regulars and some people who finished dinner and weren't quite ready to brave the cold and snow. And two FBI agents. I was about to start when I spotted Blankenship and Tajc at a table near the back.

I usually start with one of a half dozen simple tunes that allow me to judge the volume balance between voice and guitar, tunes by the Eagles, or James Taylor, or Billy Joel. Tonight, I opted for "Every Breath you Take" by the Police. I hoped the Federales got the joke. At the end of the song, they didn't clap with the rest of the audience, just stared at me with those cold hard cop eyes. They weren't drinking. Millie, one of the waitresses walked over to their table and said something I couldn't hear. Tajc flashed his badge and said something that made her back up a step as if she'd been slapped.

I normally choose songs for the first twenty minutes to feel out the crowd; see whether they are in the mood for light rock, oldies, blues, or country. I save the Gin Sing classics for late in the evening unless somebody requests one. Tonight, after "Every Step," it was Poco's "Crazy Love," my acoustic version of Smokey Robinson's "Shop Around," and Collin Raye's "That's my Story." When it came time for a blues tune, I decided to pull out one of Boley's songs from the Lewisburg session, "For You," a minor key bump and grinder that was a departure from the standard twelve-bar chord progression.

"Something bluesy for you from the late great Boley Watts." I shot a glance at the agents, and they stared back, stone faced. "A song about the perils of misinterpretation."

I adapted the song to finger style instead of Boley's heavy picking soon after I heard it. The melody was a common blues idiom, but the lyrics were stunning:

She sits at my table, drink in her hand
She points at me up on the stage, says, "Everybody, that's my man."
She don't understand, she hasn't got a clue.
Thinks I'm singin' for her, but I'm singin' for you."

I'm sittin' in the kitchen, playin' my guitar
Try to find the words to fit in the middle eight bars
She's in the next room listenin' to the birth of the blues.
Thinks I'm writin' for her, but I'm writin' for you.

It's hard to take it, the lie I gotta live,

But 'til we can make it, my song is the best I can give.

The crowd screams and whistles when I make my guitar cry
Or stroke the neck like a lover and make it sigh.
I'm pourin' out my heart, it's all I can do.
They think I'm playin' for them, but I'm playin' for you.

Through the glare of the spotlight and the cigarette haze
From the far end of the bar, I can feel your gaze.
My words reach out to you across the crowded room
They think I'm singin' for them but I'm singin' for you.

That earned me a pretty good burst of applause. I looked to Blankenship and Tajc and saw their heads together talking. And then I saw Tanner come in. He was wearing the same raincoat and hat I saw him in at my apartment. He sat at an empty table halfway to the stage where I couldn't miss him under a Corona sign. He slouched in his chair with a smug grin on his face. I made a show of tuning up a little until he ordered a drink and couldn't just stand up and walk out.

"I have a special shout-out to members of the Federal law enforcement community this evening, Agents Tajc and Blankenship of the FBI." Their heads whipped around. "You fellows need to introduce yourselves to Charles Tanner over here." I pointed him out, and he got what Collin Raye calls that "deer in the headlights" look.

"You three have a lot of interests in common."

It sounded like Tanner called me a son of a bitch under his breath, but I couldn't be sure. He stood up, threw some bills on the table, and stormed out. Blankenship and Tajc followed him with their eyes, but not their feet. I wasn't disappointed. I saw Blankenship jotting something down. They'd be reading his pedigree before morning. I was sure Tanner had a file with the Bureau, like most Americans.

As the night went on, I noticed something common over the last year or so as I looked over the crowd. Blue faces. Blue from the glow of cell phones. I've come to the conclusion that too many people come to music venues for the wrong reasons these days. They don't come to see and hear performers; they come to be seen and to take selfies to put on Facebook: Look where we are. Aren't you jealous?

I remember reading that when Bossa Nova virtuoso Charlie Byrd did a set at a club or restaurant, service stopped. No food, no drinks, no distractions until his performance was over. I wonder what he would have made of cell phones.

The rest of my gig was business as usual except for one detail. I didn't take my usual break after ninety minutes to have a beer and schmooze with the crowd. I didn't want to give Blankenship and Tajc an opening. They left during my last half hour, Tajc turning back to walk up to the stage and slip a five-dollar bill into the Mason jar I use for tips. He gave me that insincere smile of his and shot me with his forefinger. I smiled around my words and winked. I was being a wise ass, but I have to admit, he and Blankenship had me worried.

As I was packing up at the end of the night, Mark came by.

"So the FBI was here tonight, huh?"

I looked down then looked Mark in the eye and nodded. "Yeah. Sorry about that."

"I'm not worried. Nothing to hide here, but shit like that makes the patrons nervous. See what you can do so they don't come back next time." His unspoken message was, "or there won't another next time."

"I'll take care of it." I understood Mark's point. Most people, including cops, don't want cops around when they're hanging loose. It throws water on the campfire. There was no legitimate way I could keep Tajc and Blankenship from following me around. I was hopeful that they'd chase Tanner's tail for a while, and maybe by the time I came up in the rotation at Casey's again, the situation would be settled. If only.

I didn't take my guitar and gear bag to the van at first. I wanted my hands empty in case Tanner had some idea about jumping me. I could tell by his look that he was sorely pissed off that I put the Feds onto him. If he's clean, I thought, he's got no worries, but I knew better; whoever he was working for didn't want Baby to hang on a wall.

I walked out to my van and stood beside it for five minutes, my breath steaming in the cold, and realized Tanner wasn't going to pop out of the shadows. I loaded my equipment and drove to my apartment. No lights behind me. As I pulled to the curb beside my building, I saw the Feebs' car idling halfway up the block. I shut off the engine, grabbed my guitar, and headed for the entrance. For good measure, I turned and waved to Blankenship and Tajc.

Carlotta was asleep when I came in. She'd be up in three hours to go to work. I lay awake almost that long thinking about my situation and how to play it. Boley, I thought, what the hell did you get me into?

XXI

The phone rang the next morning, and the Caller ID tagged it as HMPD—Hanniston Metro Police Department. I picked up the handset, and before I could say anything, a voice at the other end greeted me with, "Sam Dunne, my favorite civilian."

"Mike Kearny." I could imagine him in his off-the-rack suit tipped back in his chair, sensible cop shoes propped on his desk.

The homicide detective laughed. "I could never be an obscene phone freak. My voice gives me away every time."

"Who died?"

"Nobody, why?

The only time you ever call me is when somebody croaks and I'm a suspect."

"Not this time; nobody's dead so far."

I knew the answer, but I asked the question anyway. "So, what's up?"

"I called because the Chief got a 'courtesy visit' from two of our cousins in the Bureau."

"Blankenship and Tajc."

"Good guess. They wanted to know all about you, so the Chief sent them to talk to me since you and I are such pals."

"And what did you tell them?"

"I told them you were an upstanding pillar of the community." Kearny's tone did a 180. "What do you think I told them? I told them you were a colossal pain in the ass who likes to cowboy up and run his own show when he ought to leave it to the professionals." He still hasn't forgiven me for shooting Danny Barton and saving his, Kearny's, life instead of the other way around.

"At least I'm consistent."

"Yeah, now you're a pain in their ass too."

"Always good to diversify."

Kearny got serious. "They didn't tell me much, but they aren't happy with you. These two could really put your nuts in a vise for obstruction if you don't play along. You might think about cooperating with them."

"Thanks for the tip. How's Devon?" Devon Wilson, Kearny's partner accented the first syllable of his name with a long E.

"Weighing his career options; stay on the force or be a model for *GQ*."

"I could never figure how he could wear a Glock and not push his suit out of shape."

"All in the cut of the coat."

"So tell me, Mike, if I talk to these guys, do I need to lawyer up?"

"Doesn't look like it from what they told me, but like I said, there wasn't much detail. The way it looks, you're more of an annoyance to them than anything, but they did request a copy of your jacket."

"I'll think about what you said."

"Word to the wise guy, Wise Guy." He hung up and left me to consider my options. I could tell them what I knew and let the Bureau's cryptography techs puzzle over the six-by-six code, or I could give them Boley's guitar with the fake pickguard and let them twist in the wind, or I could continue to stonewall, but for what? Even if I could figure out Boley's code, it might not lead to the missing money, and if it did, and I found the cash, then what? Turn it over to the Feds, or keep it? Sometimes, the smartest thing to do is stand pat and do nothing; wait and see what develops, and that was what I decided to do.

That afternoon, Carlotta came home from work with a troubled look. "Sam, something strange happened today. A customer came into Dora's and Sally waited on him, but when he was done with breakfast, he told her to call me over. He said, "Sam Dunne thinks he's funny, but we'll see who gets the last laugh." Then he got out of the booth, put on his hat and coat, and left."

"What did he look like?"

"Tall, clean-shaven, had on a pretty good suit. He looked like he was in good shape. His eyebrows were weird; they had scars in them."

"Green belted raincoat?"

Carlotta nodded.

"Charles Tanner, Private Investigator," I said, as if it were the name of a TV show. "Did he say anything else? Did he touch you?"

She shook her head. "As a matter of fact, he went out of his way to not touch me."

I told her about Tanner's persistence over buying Baby for his client and my calling him out in front of Blankenship and Tajc at Casey's. She shook her head. "You probably shouldn't have done that, Sam."

"Hell, I figured shine a light on him, and he'd scuttle back under the baseboard like the roach he is. Guess I was wrong."

Tanner was sending me a warning, an implicit threat, not from his message, but his messenger. He was letting me know he knew about Carlotta. I decided it was time to throw some sand in his gears.

XXII

Blood Lightning was playing at Bendik's that night, and that was where I would find Razor fronting the band.

Bendik's is an old factory in the East End converted into a cavernous bar patronized by bikers, outlaws, misfits, and all the other people at the fringe of Hanniston's population. It's the place people go who aren't welcome anywhere else.

I drove straight over instead of trying to shake any tail on me. Actually, I would have liked to see Tanner follow me into Bendik's, or for that matter, Blankenship and Tajc. I wonder what the gang there would have made of Tanner's belted trench coat and Sam Spade hat.

The band started at nine, so I went early. I parked in the gravel lot across the street. The usual row of Harleys was missing in front of the place because of the weather. I often wondered how bikers got around in the middle of February, and that night I figured it out. The parking lot had one of every kind of pickup truck Detroit ever made. My old Dodge Caravan looked totally out of place, like a librarian at an orgy. People think it's funny, a rock'n'roller driving a soccer mom mini-van, but it holds all my gear up to a full sound system and lights, the mileage is better than average, and it fits in a regular parking space.

I took the cash out of my wallet and split it over four pockets. The wallet I locked in the van's console. I didn't bother taking my Beretta with me. If I pulled a gun that size on anybody in Bendik's he'd laugh at me and shove it up my nose. Or she. Some of the women in the place were as mean as the guys. T

The door was flanked by a pair of bouncers whose heavy coats made them look twice their size, which was big enough already to be imposing. They knew me, and let me in without a word. I'd played in Bendik's plenty of times in the past, but every time I walked through the door from the outside world, it challenged my sense of reality.

Frankie, the usual inside doorman was MIA. He bought a bag of soap flakes instead of cocaine from some skinny kid in the projects, and when he went to get his money back, the kid panicked and peeled off the side of Frankie's face with a sawed-off .410. Can't blame the kid. Frankie went two-fifty and had a face that would scare Wes Craven.

Instead of falling down like he was supposed to, Frankie took the shotgun away from the kid, threw it away, and pounded the pusher's head to mush against a fire hydrant. I figured the guys in his old cell block would throw him a welcome home party when he got out of the hospital. I threw a five on the pile of bills for my cover and went looking for Razor.

The bar area at the front of the building was lit primarily by red neon that painted the room the color of a working foundry. The tables were more occupied than not with hard-assed men and hard-eyed women. Nobody with any brains came to Bendik's looking for a fight, but if one started, the consequences could be dire.

I passed through the bar crowd to the dance floor ringed with tables and served by a bar of its own. Heavy metal pounded from an overhead sound system wreathed in a perpetual cloud of smoke. If anyone ever tried to enforce Pennsylvania's smoking ban in Bendik's, he was wasting his time. That's where I found Razor, one hand wrapped around a long-necked Budweiser, and the other around a long-necked woman with enough tattoos to open a gallery. I leaned against the bar and waved for the waitress. Razor saw me and said something in the woman's ear. She nodded and strolled away. Razor waved me over. "Sam. How's it going?"

I told him about Tanner pestering me then following me and finally showing up at Dora's.

"I can fix that," Razor said. "I'll send Jerome to talk to him." Jerome—I don't know his last name or even if he has one—is an ex-con whose IQ is inversely proportionate to his bench-press capacity. His specialty is breaking limbs.

"No, don't send Jerome. I just want this guy off my back for a while, not dead. I have an idea." I told Razor what I wanted, and he said, "Roy's tomorrow. Late." He took a long pull on his beer. "Staying for the show?"

"Can't tonight. Got a code to crack."

He nodded. "Tomorrow then." He headed for the backstage doorway and I set my bottle unfinished on the bar. I figured the less time I spent in Bendik's the longer I'd live.

XXIII

I needed to talk with Johnny Malone for his own protection about what was happening and what he could say to the FBI to stay out of trouble if they braced him about the guitar. The store was open 'til seven on Thursdays, so I put on my jacket and headed for the van. There was almost no traffic because of the rotten weather, so it was easy for me to spot the tail. The car was about half a block behind me and made all three of the same turns I did. When I stopped at a stop sign, I hesitated just long enough for the car to pull under a street light. It was my friends in the white Buick. They either didn't have the sense or the resources to use a different car. Instead of turning south to Malone's, I turned north and headed for the library on Eighth Avenue. The Buick stayed a half block back, but it was following me as if I were pulling it by an invisible string.

When I pulled into a space in the library lot, I saw my tail slow down for a second then drive off. I figured they'd be back after a pass around the block. I made a point of standing for five minutes in the reading section in front of one of the big windows so they could see me leafing through a couple of magazines. I took off my jacket and sat in a chair away from the window to make it look as if I were dropping anchor for a while. I ducked down, grabbed my coat, and headed for the rear exit hunched over to the puzzled stare of Barry the head librarian. I just waved as I went by.

I slipped out the back door of the library and left my van out front in the parking lot. Walking to Malone's seemed to be my best bet. I figured that anybody following me would stick with the car, and if they happened to see me coming out of the back door, I could take alleys and wrong-way streets to shake them. Any footprints I left would be covered over in minutes by the drifting snow. I looked back when I turned a corner and didn't see anyone following behind.

It was dark, it was cold, and only a few cars were moving through the deepening snow. I expected the Arctic equivalent of a tumbleweed to blow across the street any minute. About three blocks away from Malone's, a movement up ahead caught my eye. A face popped out of an alley and ducked back in again. I was already leery about being followed, so I kept walking but moved away from the building side of the sidewalk to make myself a harder target. My right hand slid into my pocket and my finger curled around the end of my Beretta. From the corner of my eye I saw the reflection of a shadowy figure coming up behind me in the window of a darkened storefront.

The head popped out again, and something else, a cell phone. I tumbled to what was happening. The Knockout Game. Sucker punch a stranger on the street and try to knock him out in one shot while your friends video it for Facebook, Snapchat, or whatever platform. One more example of Social Media being the new root of all evil. The game ramped up recently.

The car made all three of the same turns I did.

Now the player didn't stop at a knockout. He had to take a hat, a glove, or some other souvenir as a trophy.

The snow muffled the sound of the punk's shoes, so I didn't hear him 'til a second before he tapped me on my left shoulder.

What he expected was for me to turn to the left to see who was behind me, making the side of my face an easy target. What he got instead was a sharp clockwise pivot ending in a left hook to his jaw with all my momentum behind it. He fell on his back in the snow like a bag of laundry. I looked toward the alley and saw the kid with the cell phone and two of his buddies staring open-mouthed at their pal on the sidewalk. I pulled one of his hundred-dollar basketball shoes off his foot.

I thought his posse might make a move on me for nailing their pal, but they took a step backward as I passed the alley, gun still at the ready in my pocket. I threw the tennis shoe at their feet and said, "Looks like I won."

I made it to Malone's about fifteen minutes before closing. Johnny was alone in the store; he'd sent Nick home hours before because of the weather. He locked the front door and shut out the showroom lights. We went back into his workshop to talk. He opened the little fridge he keeps in the corner and pulled out two bottles of Blue Rocket. Craft beers are his hobby, and he's always finding a new one with some odd name like Tire Patch or Devil's Armpit. Blue Rocket tasted like somebody dissolved an aspirin in the bottle.

"So, Sam, what kind of mess have you got yourself in this time?"

"Johnny, you won't believe it."

I laid out the whole story about the missing money, restoring the numbers on the pickguard, and all of the interested parties who were hovering around me. "I don't want you to get into hot water with the Feds, and I really don't want trouble for you from Tanner or the pair of black guys who've been following me around."

"If the Feds sniff around long enough, they'll tag me as a known associate, right?"

"Maybe. If they do, tell them I brought the guitar in for you to fix, you did, and you no longer have it. Don't lie to them. That's how they get leverage on people. Just say you no longer have the guitar."

Johnny looked at the floor and raised his eyebrows. "Okay. I'll stonewall. What's the worst they can do?"

"Give you ten to twenty for obstruction." We both laughed. He knew I was joking.

"And this other guy, Tanner?"

"He's a private eye. You don't even have to talk to him. The unknown factor is the pair who've been tailing me in an old white Buick. They aren't very subtle, but they are persistent. The FBI won't hurt you, and neither will Tanner, but these two are pretty far down the food chain, and if they get pissed off enough, who knows what they might try."

Johnny raised his shirt, and I saw the butt of a revolver sticking out of his waistband. "No worries." He jerked his head toward the showroom. "Wanna jam?"

We pulled a pair of acoustic guitars off the wall and started playing. We traded riffs for a while and for a half hour, everything else went away.

When I got back to the library, my van was still parked in the same spot under two inches of snow. I saw no tracks around it, so it was unlikely somebody was sitting in the back seat waiting for me. The white Buick was parked on the street halfway down the block. There was no steam from the exhaust. They must have been freezing, and the thought pleased me no end. I was tempted to wave but thought better of it. I took my own advice. It's never a good idea to pet a strange dog, or to kick one either. I pretended they didn't exist, cleaned the snow off my windows, and drove home with them tagging along behind me.

Later, when I told Carlotta about the Knockout Game, she said, "Good for you." Then she frowned and said. "What if the guy you nailed was under eighteen? Could you be arrested?"

"It was too dark for anybody to recognize me from a cell phone video. Besides, if they used it as evidence, they'd have to admit what they were up to."

"Better it was you than me," she said. "I'm too little to fight fair." She reached into her purse beside her on the chair. She set her two-shot .38 derringer on the table in front of her. "I'd've just shot the son-of-a-bitch."

XXIV

Tanner's veiled threat made me nervous. I decided I'd go to the diner the next day for breakfast in case he showed up again.

Dora's is one restaurant that serves old-style diner food 24-7. It's a family business, been around since the fifties, serving hot roast beef sandwiches with mashed potatoes and gravy or bacon and eggs day or night. A long counter with old-fashioned pedestal stools shares a wide aisle with a dozen booths. Diners in the booths can look out the windows and watch the traffic on 15th Street. My old girlfriend Jenny used to work there before she got lured away to Hollywood, and when Carlotta came to live with me, she took a job there doing what she does best, "waitressing."

I scanned the crowd and didn't see Tanner, but I did spot Cotton having breakfast in a booth in the back, still in his suit from the night before. He had recently shaved his head as a change of style, and it shone like polished mahogany.

I slipped into the booth across from him. He was halfway through a stack of pancakes swimming in syrup.

"Diabetes on a plate," I said.

"Sweet lips keep the ladies happy."

"Oh yeah? So how's your sax life?"

"Still gigging at the Regent." Sax to the Max was a fixture in Hanniston's nightlife.

Carlotta set a cup and saucer in front of me. "Come to sample the *haute cuisine*?" She poured without having to look and didn't spill a drop.

"And to ogle the hired help," I said with a grin.

"Ham and eggs, right?"

"She knows you too well," Cotton said around his fork.

Four guys a couple of booths nearer the door were being loud and obnoxious, and one of them, a big guy in a lumberjack shirt started mouthing off at Carlotta every time she passed their booth. "Hey, baby, why don't you come over here and squirt some milk in my coffee? I know you got some to spare."

"Why don't you put some of your own in it?"

His buddies laughed, but he didn't. "She told you, Roy," one of them said.

"Shit. Wait'll she comes back."

Cotton lifted an eyebrow. I shook my head. "She's a big girl. She'll handle it."

When Carlotta passed the booth again with a coffee pot in her hand, Roy leaned out and reached up under her skirt, grabbing at her ass. Carlotta swung the stainless steel carafe and caught him on the side of the head with it, knocking him back into the booth. She took a step past Cotton and me and planted her feet, ready to defend herself.

"My turn."

I stood up and put myself between Roy and Carlotta. He snarled at me. "You got a problem, asshole?"

"No, but you might."

He swung a roundhouse at me, and I ducked it, stepping in to give him a hard shot to his gut. The air whooshed out of him and he doubled over. I grabbed him by the hair and brought his head down on my knee. He fell backward, nose spraying blood. His pals were scrambling out of the booth ready to collectively kick my ass when they suddenly froze. Cotton's forearm was over my shoulder, a .38 in his hand, aimed at Roy's posse. "Time to pay your check and go, gentlemen," he said. "And don't forget to tip your waitress."

"Another time, pal," one of them said, pushing his chin out at me.

"Why wait?" My left hand shot out and caught a handful of his face. I spun him and slammed his forehead on the counter. He staggered back, dazed.

"Anybody else?" I said.

End of argument. Roy's buddies half carried him out the door.

"You didn't really need to do that," I told Cotton. "I could've handled it."

"Yeah, but why wreck the diner? I like Dora's. I'd hate to be blackballed."

"That would be redundant. If you'd've fired that gun next to my ear, you'd've made me deaf."

He laughed. "Might improve your music."

XXV

I went into Roy's that evening just after six and found Razor in the same booth where I'd found him before. This time, he was alone. I slid into the booth and ordered a beer.

Razor pulled out a deck of cards and shuffled them. "Ante up." I threw some money down beside his. He grinned. "Cut for twenty?"

I cut the deck and pulled a ten of diamonds. Razor cut and pulled a two of spades. He pushed a twenty from his pile onto mine. "Again?" I cut for a six of hearts and he pulled a ten of clubs. I slid a twenty from my pile across the table and he nodded. "Another one?" By the time we were done, I had eight bogus bills and he had sixty dollars of mine. If anybody saw the transaction, they'd pass it off as a friendly card game. Razor grinned. "Double or nothing?"

"I think I'll quit while I'm ahead." We finished our beers while Bruce Springsteen bellowed about being born to run. Razor stood and held up his hand, spreading the fingers. I nodded and waited for five minutes before I walked out of Roy's in case anybody was parked outside watching the door. I started the van and drove away slowly, taking the straight route to my apartment. I saw the same headlights in my rearview mirror the whole way, and when I parked in front of my building, the headlights pulled up to the curb a half block away.

I gave it a minute before I got out of the car and as I stepped into the lights under the building's portico, I pulled my keys out of my jacket, letting the packet of twenties land on the sidewalk. I made like I didn't notice and let myself into the building, hoping Tanner was watching me with a good pair of binoculars.

Inside, I went to the super's office and rapped on the door. Jerry answered in pajamas and a bathrobe. I could hear gunfire and screeching tires from the cop show he was watching on TV. "What's up, Sam?"

"Need a favor, Jerry. Can I watch the security cams for a minute?"

He rolled his eyes. I held out a twenty—a real one, and he stepped back from the doorway. "Come on in." He led me down the hallway to the closet-sized room where he kept the alarm system and the security monitors. Shadows danced in the flickering blue light from the three screens. The camera under the portico showed nothing for a few minutes. Lights from a few passing cars splashed on the sidewalk. I was beginning to think that Tanner wasn't watching closely enough when I saw him step into frame. He stopped on the sidewalk, setting one foot on the folded money. He lit a cigarette as an excuse for stopping, cupping his hand around his lighter. He dropped it, and when he stooped to pick it up, scooped up the bills. He shoved them into his pocket with the lighter and walked away.

"Got you."

Jerry blinked. "Huh?"

"Oh, nothing. Thanks, Jerry. I saw what I needed to see. Go back to your cop show."

It might take a day, but if luck was on my side, Tanner would be out of my hair pretty soon.

The next day, a liquor store owner and a guy who ran a deli on 14th Street went yelling to the cops about a guy passing bad twenties. Tanner's face was on the security video from the liquor store, and it took Hanniston's finest less than a day to track him down with two of the counterfeit bills still in his wallet. He'd be off the street for a day or two, and I'd breathe a little easier in Florida.

XXVI

had two choices to get to Florida, fly or drive. I could get cheap air fares on line with Spirit, but shipping my gear would cost a bundle, and I have never trusted airline baggage handlers with my guitars. A thousand miles?" Carlotta said, "You'll get killed on the gas."

"I'd agree, but Jensen Beach has no airport to land a passenger jet, so we'd have to fly to Orlando or Lauderdale and pay a limo driver a hundred bucks to take us to Jensen and another hundred or so to drive us back to the airport at the end of the week." I didn't even have to flip a coin. Carlotta worked out the days off with Dora's, we packed our bags and drove away from Hanniston as fast as the snowy roads would let us.

I split the drive to Jensen Beach over two days. I used to drive to Florida in one sixteen-hour shot, but the older I get, the more I appreciate taking my time. Besides, I had Carlotta with me, so the company was worth the extra day. I asked her if she wanted to take a side jaunt to Myrtle Beach, and go see some of her friends, but she nixed the idea. "There aren't really that many people in Myrtle I'd want to see. Nobody close, anyway."

So we left Sunday to arrive Tuesday and give me a day to rest up before the gig. We drove, and drove, and drove. We listened to a Lee Child Jack Reacher novel on the CD player, and when that was done, to get into the Florida mood, we switched to Tim Dorsey's *Florida Roadkill.* I laughed so hard at the adventures of Serge and Coleman and that poor deluded metal head Dar-Dar that at one point halfway through Georgia I almost bounced the Caravan off the Jersey barrier. Carlotta told me to pull over and switch. "If I'm going to die in a car crash," she said, "I don't want it to be because of your sense of humor."

We pulled into Jensen Beach near five Tuesday afternoon. After we checked into our room at the Holiday Inn, I drove over to Roland's to unload my equipment. I try to avoid leaving any of my gear in the van in a strange place. Too many brigands out there.

Roland's was right on the beach sandwiched between two monumental high-rise hotels. I could just hear the grinding of teeth among developers who'd like to plant a third one just like them on what was a primo piece of real estate. The restaurant was a good thirty years old, built to look like an oversized wharf shack complete with pilings joined with chain links the size of my hand. People were waiting in line to get inside.

Ted Martin, the manager of Roland's was one of those fresh-faced under thirty types with a trendy haircut who wore a white shirt and a necktie like a small-town sheriff wears gold braid or stars on his epaulets to let you know he's in charge. The Peter Principle in the flesh. I later met Roland White, the owner and the real boss, who spent most of his time behind a desk in the office in sweat pants and a T-shirt.

Ted shook my hand and gave it a squeeze. I was tempted to put on the pressure and grind his bones together, but I let it go. I figured, why give it away. People who try to intimidate with a bone-crushing grip are often compensating for some inadequacy, like cowardice; that or they're trying to scare potential aggressors away like a Siamese Fighting Fish spreading its fins and doubling its size. Either way, I wasn't impressed. "So, Ted, where can I store my equipment?"

"Come on out to the bar." He led me through a busy table section filled with diners and through a double glass door. The beachside lounge was a covered flagstone patio with a full wet bar and tables set up to serve at least fifty people. The decor was consistent with the facade, maintaining the fishing chic motif. Anchors, buoys, nets, and lobster traps were carefully placed by some decorator with an eye for impact. The lighting was subdued; most of it coming from fixtures styled to look like antique lanterns. It was six o'clock and at least half of the tables were occupied. The platform Roland's used as a stage put my back to the ocean, which I could hear occasionally between the songs blaring from the overhead speakers. Overhead I saw the lighting system, a set of pots with colored gels run by a rank of dimmers behind the stage. They looked adequate, so I wouldn't need to use my own.

"We're a little busy right now, so if you don't mind, we'd like you to wait 'til later to bring it through. We don't like to disturb the patrons."

"Understood. What time are we talking?"

"After eleven." I was liking this twit less every minute.

He led me through the tables to a back room behind the bar. It was stacked with everything a working bar needed except the alcohol. "You can put it in here for now. You'll be leaving it set up for the whole five days, right?"

"If it storms, a good wind will blow the rain right under the eaves and soak everything."

"We have pull-down doors, the same ones we use at closing time, to take care of that."

I shook my head. "I'll tear down every night when I'm done."

Ted frowned. "Well, the bar will still have patrons then. We don't want you to—"

"Disturb them by carrying equipment through." I finished for him. "If I leave it set up, does your insurance cover loss by theft for contractors?"

I got the feeling nobody ever asked him the question before. "I'll have to check with Mr. White." I got the impression that like most middle managers, Ted had to check with the boss—not the manager, the owner—every time he blew his nose. I was getting a really clear picture of the power structure.

"Tell you what, Ted," I said. "I'll leave my stuff set up if you'll sign a form personally guaranteeing its repair or replacement in case of theft or damage." I didn't bother to tell him I already had it insured.

"I—I don't have the authority," he stammered.

"Then go ask your boss." From the look on his face, I might as well have told him to stick his hand in a box full of scorpions.

"It's been a long day driving, Ted. Can I just put my stuff in the closet?"

"Uh, sure. Go ahead."

"We can sort out this business about night-to-night tear down later."

I didn't wait for an answer. I went out to the van and started loading the dolly.

When I got back to the room, Carlotta was fresh out of the shower and propped up on the king-sized bed watching *The Fast and the Furious* on the big-screen TV.

"How many times have you seen that movie?" I said.

"Maybe ten, maybe twelve. Who's counting?"

"I don't see what's so great about it. All Vin Diesel does is walk around and grunt."

"Yeah, but he's hot."

"Should be a category in the Oscars."

"You're just jealous."

She was right. The next morning I put on my swimsuit to go with Carlotta to the beach and checked myself out in the mirror. "What's Vin Diesel got that I don't?"

"It's more like what do you have that he doesn't?" she said, grabbing me around the waist.

"If I had a team of trainers, dieticians, and coaches to keep me ripped, I'd look the same as him."

"Not even if you shaved your beard and your head."

I slapped her on the backside and said, "Come on, bathing beauty. Let's go out on the beach and see how I stack up against the local talent."

Jensen Beach, like most of the mid-coast Florida beaches, is warm, but the water can vary, depending on the currents flowing from the North. Today, it was about seventy degrees, and the sun shone. The water was in the low sixties, but we went in anyway, remembering it was eighteen degrees back home. Everything's relative.

The crowd on the beach was a little thin, but it was a weekday and school was in. I was surprised at the number of people on the beach who spoke anything but English, sometimes whole clans of twenty or more staying at the beachfront hotels. I was surprised too at the number of people who brought their dogs, not just to the beach, but on vacation at all. Some of them seemed to be enjoying themselves but some of them, tethered to a beach umbrella or a lounge chair, seemed absolutely miserable.

Lying in the sun on an oversized beach towel pushed Baby, the missing money, the FBI, and Tanner to the back of my mind, but I knew Carlotta was thinking about it. She said, "Do you think Tanner or those agents followed us down here?"

"They're fools if they didn't if just for the weather. I doubt Tanner's expense account could cover a Florida junket. And if the Feds are still that interested in me, they have agents all over, including Florida. They'll just put someone local on the case. Besides, they can track my cell phone and the E-Z Pass transponder in the van."

"You just can't get away anymore," Carlotta said, almost wistfully.

She was right. Cell phone triangulation, e-mail login, security cameras everywhere, ATM records, fingerprint and DNA databases. A crook doesn't have much of a chance when a murderer kills somebody in Pittsburgh and the cops can find and arrest him four days later in Sacramento. "I figure that all this high-tech police procedure will be the death of the detective novel."

"What do you mean, Sam?"

"Somebody's murdered and the investigators find a partial license plate in a security cam image from a Dunkin' Donuts three blocks away. They run the partial plate and the car's description through a DMV database and narrow it down to a half dozen possible vehicles and figure out by the Turnpike transponders which was where when. They get a name and an address, and the computer tech hacks into the electric company database and sees by the spike in his current power usage that the perp's home. Then they use Google Maps and aerial photos to determine the best ways to approach the location, send in the SWAT team and it's all wrapped up before lunch."

Carlotta was laughing at my indignation. "You almost sound as if you're rooting for the bad guys."

I shook my head. "No way. I just like the idea of detectives actually detecting to solve crimes, find out who did what the old way; shoe leather and occasionally beating it out of somebody. I'll take Sam Spade or Marlowe over any of these high-tech cops any day."

"Sam," Carlotta said with a straight face, "You're such a romantic."

I went in at four thirty to set up my gear for the first night at Roland's. Six to nine was a time slot that looked better to me every year I aged. Playing 'til two in the morning drains you. When you're young, you bounce back quickly. The older you get, the slower you bounce.

I was ready to do a sound check when Roland White walked onto the patio, and the whole staff seemed to snap to attention. Turns out I was right about him. He was the kind of boss who made all the substantial decisions and kept a staff of gerbils around to report to him and do his bidding.

"You're Sam Dunne." He put one foot onto the platform and held out his hand. "I'm Roland White." He looked about ten years younger than his real age because of a trim build, a cultivated sun tan, and a full head of thick, blond hair.

"Pleased to meet you."

His handshake was firm but not a bone crusher. He was confident in his authority and didn't need to physically intimidate anyone. "Do you have everything you need?"

"Yes. I'm pretty much self-contained."

"If you do need anything, just leave me a note. I can't trust these damned kids I hire to take care of anything properly."

Maybe that's because you never give them a chance to do it, I thought. "I don't imagine there'll be any problems."

"The agent sent me a demo. You have a pretty good variety of material."

"Thanks. I try to have something for every taste. Anything but rap, opera, and speed metal."

White surprised me by laughing; I took him for the humorless sort. "You'll fit in well with our crowd, mostly over thirty, business and professional types."

"I'll find something they like."

"I'm sure you will." He stepped back to the bar and leaned against it while I plugged in my guitar and switched on my system. I strummed a few chords and tweaked the EQ. White said something to the bartender, a young girl with blond hair the consistency of Borkum Riff pipe tobacco, and she hustled to shut off the piped-in music.

I tapped the mic and said, "Coming to you live." The cliche is "Check one two." That usually gets a response from some clown fish in the crowd like, "Three four—I can count too. Yuk yuk." The P.A. system fed back a little in the outdoor setting. I adjusted the mid-range, and the problem went away. I shot a picture of the drawbar and knob settings with my cell phone so that I could restore them quickly if some prankster moved them when I wasn't around.

There are a few standard tunes I play for sound checks, songs I'm accustomed to hearing myself do. I can play and sing them on autopilot and focus on sound. I know how they should sound, and I can hear what adjustments need to be made.

I opted this time for Don McClean's "Castles in the Air." The sound was good in spite of the bounce back from the stone floor and the wall of the building. I shut things down and stepped off the platform. Roland White was still at the bar. I give him credit for sticking around to hear the whole song.

"What song was that you played?" he asked.

"'Castles in the Air'. It's a Don McClean song.

"Oh, the 'American Pie' guy."

At the same time I envied his success. I always felt sorry for McClean. He said once in an interview, that he was tired of playing "American Pie," but it was what people paid to hear him sing night after night. McClean to me was analogous to George Reeves as Superman on TV. Yeah, "American Pie" is a great song, but to let it shove aside his other songs, beauties like "Castles" and "Vincent" is an injustice to his talent.

"He writes a lot of good material. You should give it a listen some time."

"Yeah. Maybe I will. Well, got work to do. Talk to you later, Dunne." And he was gone. Yeah, talk *to* me, not *with* me, a distinction that's lost on too many people.

Carlotta went with me the first night at Roland's and sat at a table halfway back from the stage. She's not what most people would call a classic beauty, but she always looks good in a sexy way, and she definitely has class. Tonight, she wore a white peasant blouse over a pleated skirt with sandals that showed off her toes. Her skin was that delicate shade of light sunburn the first day at the beach always gives her. Tomorrow, it would darken into a rich dusky gold.

I pointed her out to the bartender and told him to run a tab.

Six o'clock arrived, and I went on stage. I floated a few standard acoustic numbers to feel out the crowd. They were more responsive than audiences I've had elsewhere. There are lots of nights when I feel like I'm nothing but live Muzak as a background for their conversations, but this crowd actually paid attention to what I was doing. I went to some originals, and they were well received too. The place was turning out to be better than I expected.

The first hour and into the second, people were sitting for a song or two and leaving when those little red light buzzers the hostess gave them went off to announce that their tables were ready. Past that point, more people came in after dinner for drinks and dropped anchor. I had a nearly full house the last hour, and they were a pretty good crowd.

People started yelling requests, and I was glad to play them. I don't have as broad a repertoire as my friend Ricky Stover who bills himself as a human jukebox, but I can chase down chords and lyrics of most songs people request with my I-pad. If I know the tune, I can manage a passable version of nearly any pop song. The tip jar filled up as the evening wore on, and at quitting time I did two encores. It looked like Roland's was going to work out.

I tore down my equipment and hauled it to the store room. I was careful not to disturb any of the patrons and to tell you the truth, I don't think anyone even noticed but Ted.

"Hungry?" I asked Carlotta as we walked back to the hotel.

"Yeah, I am. Let's try this place." She pointed to the neon sign up ahead that flashed Cappy's Diner.

"Looks good to me."

Cappy's Diner was snuggled up to a Starbucks/Ben & Jerry's duplex, both still open but not as busy as Cappy's at this hour. I could see a full counter as we passed the windows, and when we went inside, there was only one booth vacant. The place was tricked out in 50s chic, with Formica table tops, and red and white Naugahyde diamonds upholstering the seats. A jukebox in one corner blasted out pre-Beatles Top-40, and the walls were decorated with framed posters of movies like *Rebel Without a Cause, The Wild One, and Teenagers from Outer Space.* The general atmosphere was chaos, with waitresses hustling from the serve window to the customers and everyone talking loud to be heard over the kitchen clatter, and Little Richard singing "Good Golly Miss Molly". In other words, our kind of place.

The place was turning out to be better than I expected.

We sat in the booth and checked out the menus. I was starved, so I opted for the steak and fries combo. Carlotta decided she was hungry enough for the same meal. A cute waitress in a classic pink rayon uniform with a name tag that identified her as Dottie set down two glasses of water and pulled an order pad from under her apron.

"That's a rare name these days," Carlotta said. "Does it stand for Dorothy?"

The waitress grinned. "It stands for Courtney. Bob the owner wants us to look authentic, so he gives everybody badges with fantasy 50s names. She pointed to two waitresses at the far end of the room. That's Alicia and Taylor—Dixie and Buffy. You get the idea. We trade every few days; it keeps the creeps from knowing who we really are."

Carlotta nodded agreement. "Believe me, hon, there have been plenty of days I wished my real name wasn't stitched on my tit."

Dottie nodded, acknowledging a fellow member of the club. "So what'll you have?"

The steak was thick and tender. I was halfway through mine when I remembered I hadn't called Joe to let him know I got in okay and that the gig was working out. I reached for my cell phone and decided it didn't jibe with the Cappy's ambiance. It would keep.

"Roland's seems like a pretty nice place," Carlotta said around a bite of steak.

"Not bad, but the atmosphere's a little edgy. Roland White's management strategy seems to be to keep everybody running scared. It helps that all of his employees are kids with little experience at dealing with bullies."

"You mean he roughs them up?"

"No, it's psychological. He's more like the principal of a high school than a business owner. Everybody's afraid of his displeasure."

"Except you."

"Except me." I popped one of those thick slab fries into my mouth and chewed it a while. "I'm not a kid, and he hasn't even tried."

"Maybe he reads you well and knows better. Let's hope he doesn't. You're fighting enough battles already."

We finished our meals around half past twelve and walked to the Holiday Inn. The night was mild and the breeze off the ocean ruffled Carlotta's hair. I fished out my phone and turned it on. I usually leave it off when I'm playing a job. There's nothing more distracting than having it ring, or even buzz in my pocket while I'm trying to focus on my performance. I think of that as short-changing the audience on my attention and my professionalism. Two calls from Joe Mancini and one from a cell phone number I didn't recognize.

I thumbed the number for voice mail. The first message was from Joe. "Sam, no word from you. Everything okay? Call me." The second was Joey again. "Don't give me an ulcer. Call me, damn it."

The third was Jerry. His tone was anything but jovial. "Uh, Sam, there's been a problem at the building. Give me a call as soon as you get this." A problem? If he said a fire, a flood, anything specific, it would have been better than a generic word that left my imagination to fill in the blanks. Feeling the helplessness that hits when trouble strikes and you're too far away to do anything about it, I hit the return call icon and in a minute, Jerry answered his cell phone.

"Hello, Sam?" He was wide awake. Normally he was out cold by ten o'clock.

"Yeah, Jerry, what's up?"

"About an hour ago we had a break-in, or I should say attempted break-in. Your place."

XXVII

Jerry told me that two men forced the lock on the street door to the foyer and went up the fire stairs to my floor. They worked the lock on my apartment door with a crowbar and were just going inside when the elevator door opened and Sue and Ricky, my neighbors saw them. Ricky did the sensible thing and punched the button for the lobby instead of confronting them. He called 911 on his cell phone and got back on the elevator.

"It's lucky Sue and Ricky came when they did. According to the cops, another few seconds, and the burglars would have been inside with the door shut, and who knows what they would have grabbed."

Carlotta tugged at my sleeve. "What's wrong, Sam?"

"Somebody tried to break into the apartment, but they didn't get in. It's all right." I could tell from her expression that she didn't agree.

"I want you to do something for me, Jerry."

"Sure, Sam, what?"

"Go in the apartment with your cell phone and take pictures of each room. Send them to my phone. I want to see if anything's missing or disturbed."

"Like I said, Sam, they didn't get in —"

"You said they were going in. Maybe they were going back in. Just do it for me, Jerry, all right?"

"Okay, Sam. I'll do it now. And I'll have the carpenter in here tomorrow to fix the door frame."

"One more thing, Jerry. Did you catch these guys on the security cam in the foyer?"

"Yeah, but the cops took the tape."

"Did you see them on the video?"

"Yeah. They were two black dudes. Had their faces covered but not their hands."

My tag-alongs in the beat-up Buick. That ruled out Tajc and Blankenship. They couldn't be pros doing a burglary with bare hands. "Thanks for letting me know, Jerry. If the cops need a statement from me, tell them I'll be back in town Tuesday."

"Okay, Sam. I'll get those pictures to you right away." He hung up, and I stared at the phone for a minute.

I told Carlotta everything Jerry told me, and she just nodded and said. "Never a dull moment."

A half-hour later, my phone buzzed with a text from Jerry. Pictures coming. One by one, the thumbnails appeared on the screen of my phone. Not wanting to delay the process, I waited 'til they were done arriving, eight in all, before I enlarged the first. I studied each and handed the camera to Carlotta so that she could take a look. The first shot of the living room showed the wall with my instruments, none missing. A second angle showed my desk and bookshelves, again nothing out of place. The kitchen, bathroom, and bedroom all looked normal, as if nothing had been disturbed. A final shot showed the door frame in the hall, the wood splintered around the lock.

"We were lucky," Carlotta said.

"And the irony is, what they wanted wasn't even there."

"Boley's guitar?"

"What else?"

There was nothing either of us could do from a thousand miles away except hope that the pair didn't try again, at least until I was back in Hanniston. I had no compunction about shooting both of them dead as soon as they came through the door, and neither would Carlotta.

That night, we lay in bed. Neither of us spoke, and neither of us slept for hours. Finally, Carlotta rolled on her side and draped an arm across my chest. I twined her fingers in mine, she nestled her chin in the crook of my shoulder, and we finally drifted off to sleep.

XXVIII

We agreed the next day that we wouldn't even talk about the break-in. We had a quick breakfast at the hotel and headed for the beach. I wasn't totally burnt, but I could feel that gritty discomfort when I turned my neck or hunched my shoulders. That and the tops of my feet rubbing the tongues of my tennis shoes. Today was definitely a sunblock day. Carlotta coated me with SPF 50, and I rubbed her back and shoulders with Panama Jack til she shone like a piece of varnished oak.

We sat on the beach in the early afternoon, drank wine coolers, and enjoyed the human panorama. No secrets on the beach, unless you're wearing a burka.

I was dozing in my chair when I heard a dog barking frantically and a whirring sound like a weed eater. About twenty feet away, some lard ass in board shorts and a tank top that didn't quite make it to his navel was buzzing a chocolate Lab with a drone. I guess the high-pitched whine of the motors hurt his ears. The jerk would swoop the drone down as if he were attacking the dog then fly just out of reach as the Lab yapped and frantically tried to pull it out of the air. The dog was tied to an unoccupied beach umbrella, and the whole scene reminded me of bear baiting in the Dark Ages.

I got out of my chair and walked up behind the drone idiot. "That your dog?"

He ignored me, so I said it again. "Is that your dog?"

He still didn't look at me. "No, is he yours?" The dog was barking furiously now, jumping and snapping at the drone.

"Nope, but if you don't stop tormenting him, I'm gonna take that controller away from you, fly your drone out to sea and drop it in the water, and shove that control box up your ass." Finally, I had his attention. "Leave the dog alone, and take your toy someplace else while you still can, fat boy."

He stared at me as if I were from Mars. He thumbed the control and the drone rose. He seemed to be pondering whether to buzz me with the damned thing but thought better of it. He walked away muttering something that sounded like "glass bowl."

"Defender of the downtrodden," Carlotta said as I sat back in my chair.

"No, preserver of peace and quiet."

We didn't talk about it, but each of us knew what was on the other's mind all day. That night, Carlotta opted to stay in for the evening while I worked Roland's.

The crowd seemed to ebb and flow the same as the night before, coming and going as tables were ready and settling in for the last ninety minutes. I sold a half dozen CDs at the end of the night. *Requiem* made the charts a few years ago, but people still bought copies when I had them out for sale. Some of my friends sign the covers of their CDs in advance, but I always believed that part of the kick in buying a CD from the artist is having him or her sign it on the spot, and if the buyer wants it, to personalize the signature. Something to brag about along with a selfie with an arm around me. I didn't see Roland White Saturday, but Ted told me the boss was "satisfied" with the job I was doing. High praise from the tyrant.

Carlotta was still awake when I got back to the room. "Hungry?" she said.

"As always."

"I called room service an hour ago. Your Reuben ought to arrive any minute now. I get the pickle."

"Sigmund Freud, call your office."

XXIX

Sunday I was set to sing "The Star-Spangled Banner" at First Data Field, the spring training home of the New York Mets. I've never been a rah-rah baseball fan. I don't like to watch baseball, football, or for that matter any sport on television, but I do like to go to the ballpark a couple of times a year, sit in the cheap seats with a beer and a hot dog and enjoy the live performance—not just the players, but the people around me. I don't like some program director deciding what's important or interesting or entertaining for me. I want to watch what I want to watch.

First Data Field is located ten miles inland from Jensen Beach in a mid-sized city named Port St. Lucie. That's the city Rush Limbaugh uses as an alternate for abuse instead of Rio Lindo, as in, "He is definitely pecunious; for those of you in Port St. Lucie, that means he's rich." Highway 1 and Interstate 95 run through it on the way to Fort Lauderdale and Miami, and it's a community of five-lane roads, strip malls, and gated enclaves catering to senior citizens. The field itself is pretty nice, fashioned after an old-style ballpark complete with a good-sized bleacher section from right field to center that bakes in the afternoon sun.

Carlotta argued with me over what I should wear. She said blue jeans and a T-shirt were too casual. I said khakis and a Hawaiian shirt would make me look like I lived there instead of being fancy imported talent. We compromised on the Jimmy Buffet autograph model flowered shirt over my faded jeans.

The P.R. rep for the stadium was a thirty-something named Mariah Smith, an ambulatory suntan who would turn into a road map of lines and creases in a few years if she didn't watch herself. She was very professional and greeted me with the patented public relations smile and handshake. "We're very happy to have you with us, Mr. Dunne. According to the information Mr. Mancini sent us, you are a singer-songwriter and you were once a member of the band Gin Sing. Is that how you'd like to be introduced?"

I grinned. "No hiding from the past, is there?" At least Joe didn't mention I'd killed Danny Barton. "That will do just fine, and please call me Sam." The gig included two box seats, so Carlotta headed that direction while I unpacked my guitar. Mariah told me there would be no sound check. I would go on cold.

"Will one microphone do for you?"

"I should be able to hear myself well enough to adjust my stance after about two bars."

"Last week we had the Cub Scouts, and you could hardly hear them."

At least it wasn't an RV show.

I was surprised that the stadium filled as quickly as it did. By game time, most of the seats were filled, including the griddle seats in right field. I didn't think the Mets would be so big a draw in Florida then I reminded myself that probably half the population of Port St. Lucie had migrated there from New York and Jersey. The Jumbotron flashed pictures, stats, and trivia about the Mets and their opponent *du jour,* the Atlanta Braves. Out on the field, the players were doing their warm up drills, and to the side, pitchers were warming up in the bullpens. I never followed the Mets or the Braves, so when they flashed the players on the big screen, they were all strangers to me.

Mariah came with a wireless microphone in one hand and a mic in a tripod stand in the other. "All set?"

"Yes, Ma'am."

She walked me out to Home Plate and switched on the mic. No feedback, which was a good sign. She made a little welcoming speech over the hand-held as the teams lined up on either baseline. I heard it twice because of the classic ballpark echo. She read my pedigree and said, "Now, ladies and gentlemen, please rise for the National Anthem.

I stepped out of the shade and up to the mic, feeling the Florida sun cooking my scalp through my hair. I walked out to polite applause, expecting some yahoo in the crowd to yell, "Play Free Bird," but I was spared that cliché. I tilted the mic to what I hoped was the right angle to pick up the guitar as well as it did my voice. *A Capella* isn't my thing. I suppose you could say in a case like that one the guitar's a crutch, but I prefer to think of it as a collaborator.

I had worked up a brief instrumental intro to allow me to hear the volume and avoid confusion with the echo, which sounded like the world's longest digital delay. I got through that okay and started to sing. I got through the first two lines, looked around at the crowd, and stopped. There was an uncomfortable silence that gave way to shuffling and murmuring.

I waited roughly a full minute and leaned into the microphone. "I didn't forget the words, folks," my voice boomed and echoed. "There's a reason these men lined up along the base lines are holding their hats in their hands." Anybody with a hat on your head, take it off and show some respect, damn it."

I looked back at Mariah. Her suntan looked bleached. Her mouth hung open.

There was a little nervous laughter, then a smattering of applause that finally grew into a bigger ovation than I got when I walked onto the field. When it died, I nodded and said, "Now, let's try it again."

At the end of the song, I walked off the field to an ovation (they were already standing anyway) and nodded to Mariah, whose expression said Murder. "Sorry about that. I just looked at the crowd and it hit me the wrong way."

She didn't say a word. I took my guitar with me to the seat and had to sit with it across my and Carlotta's feet. "Well C., did I mess up?"

She laughed. "I think the game will go on as usual."

From behind me, a white-haired man in a flowered shirt tapped me on the shoulder. "You did good, son. People need to hear that once in a while." Joe Mancini would probably want to kill me, but that old man's comment made it all worthwhile.

Spring training games are fun to watch. Besides the seasoned team pros, you get to see the rookies find their bearings. Sometimes it looks almost like a sandlot game with errors all over the place. After four innings the Braves were down six runs. They had put in three pitchers, and the last did something I've never seen in a ball game: he walked four men in a row. The crowd loved it. Then the tide turned and the Braves caught up. The Mets squeaked by ten-to-nine, and the fans went home happy. As we walked out of the stadium, more than one person stopped to high-five me or tell me I did a good job.

I turned my phone on. No calls. "I guess Mariah Smith hasn't called Joe yet," I said.

"Either that or he's thumbing through the dictionary to find the right names to call you."

"Believe me, he's got plenty of his own."

XXX

Carlotta came with me for the final night of my stand at Roland's. Nobody said a word about my performance at First Data Field; I figured word hadn't gotten around yet. I was annoyed that people were playing with their cell phones more than usual. When I took a break, a table with two couples waved me over. "Have you seen this?" one of the women said, holding up her phone.

YouTube. There I was in all my glory, snarling at the boorish fans.

"You're a celebrity, Sam."

I nodded, smiled, and headed for Carlotta's table.

"What's the matter?"

"I'm a star on YouTube."

"The ballpark?"

I nodded. "Not only is Joe going to kill me, he'll have a doctor standing by to revive me so he can kill me again."

When my cell phone rang later that night, I saw Joe's name on the caller ID. I braced myself for the tirade. "Hi, Joe. I guess you heard."

"Yeah, I heard and I saw. Somebody videoed you with a cell phone and put it on Facebook."

"And—"

His voice switched gears from somber to enthusiastic "It went viral. Ninety-three percent approval, Sam. I couldn't buy that kind of publicity."

Only in America.

XXXI

Carlotta and I agreed to do the drive home in one day. It would be exhausting, but I wanted to get back to Hanniston and get a handle on the situation. Razor still had Baby hidden away, and that much was under control, but I didn't know what Tanner, the agents, or the men who broke into my apartment were up to.

I set the cruise control on the Caravan to 70 and tried to relax. It broke my heart to leave Florida in the middle of February, but life intrudes. Carlotta was curled up in the passenger seat doing a crossword puzzle. "What's an eight-letter word for recalcitrant?"

"You're kidding. You mean you don't know?"

She laughed. "Of course *I* know, the question is, do *you* know?"

"Defiant?" I counted letters in my head. "No, that's seven. Difficult? No, that's nine." I thought for a minute. "Contrary!"

"You got it. I figured you'd know, since recalcitrant means having a bad attitude toward authority or discipline."

"The lady has my number."

"Yeah, I —" She stopped in mid-sentence.

"Sam, I just thought of something." She sat up straight in the seat. "Boley left you his guitar, but what else did he leave you?"

"His watch, his lighter."

She punched my arm. "The crossword books. Maybe the six-by-six code matches up with something in the puzzles."

I upped the cruise control to eighty.

We spent most of the ride working out possibilities, ways to apply the code that might lead to one thing or another.

"Boley said he was losing his memory. Maybe he used the crossword magazines to help him remember."

"Yeah, Sam, but how is the question."

"Do you think Boley did the puzzles 'til he found the words he wanted then he quit?"

Carlotta shook her head. "That would make it too easy for anybody to pick up the magazine and just see where he stopped. I'd guess he did more puzzles beyond the one that had a specific word he wanted."

"Those puzzle magazines have the answers in the back, don't they?"

"Yeah, they do."

"Maybe he didn't even do the puzzles at all. Maybe he found the puzzle that had the right word and just filled in the answers around it."

She nodded. "Maybe so, but which puzzle and which word?"

"You know what, C.?"

"What, Sam?"

"I think Boley Watts was a lot smarter than anybody thought, me included."

"I think you're absolutely right."

We didn't get back to Hanniston 'til almost three in the morning. Heavy snow slowed us down the last leg of the drive, and we were too tired to even think, let alone try to solve a conundrum like Boley's code. Since we came back a day early, Carlotta didn't have to go to work in the morning. We could get a good night's sleep and start fresh.

XXXII

Carlotta woke first; of the two of us, she was always the early riser. I dragged myself out of bed at about eight-thirty to find her leafing through the crossword magazines at the coffee table. A sheet of paper with the code block on it beside them. "Coffee's done. Grab a cup and pour me one too, would you Sam?" She held out her mug.

"Waiting on the waitress," I chuckled.

"I'm off-duty." She leaned back and rubbed her eyes. "I woke up at five same as usual."

"Old habits are hard to break."

"But I think I may have made a break in the code."

"So tell me."

"Coffee first."

I poured two mugs and brought them back to the sofa.

"Well, what is it?"

"More like what it's not. I figured Boley didn't have access to a GPS or any detailed maps or computer programs that would give him latitude and longitude readings for a specific place. Then I started looking at number frequency like I use letter frequency to solve cryptograms; E and T are the most frequent letters, for example."

"That's why they're the single dot and dash in Morse code."

She nodded. "That's right. So, look at the 36 digits. What numbers occur the most often?"

I studied the block of numbers, counting them in my head. "One and four."

"Right. There are nine ones and six fours. Now apply them to the letters in the alphabet, first and fourth."

"A and D. Maybe the coffee hasn't kicked in yet. I'm missing something subtle here."

"A and D," she said. "Across and Down." Look at the sixth column."

"Holy shit."

She handed me the sheet with the number block.

827154
143081
922311
931164
641044
537461

"The sixth number in each row is either a four or a one. That's consistent with Across and Down."

"And the other five numbers in each row?"

"Let's look at the numbers another way besides alphabetical substitution. Months of the year one through twelve, January through December."

I looked closely at the block of numbers. "I see a ten and two elevens, no twelve. The rest would be single digits."

"Did you read across left to right, or right to left?"

"Left to right. Right to left, you lose the ten. There goes October."

"If that's the way they were intended to be read."

"Maybe there's no November or December. What if the zero is meant to stand for ten?"

"Good point."

"So if you read it right to left, the fifth line could be four October."

"Maybe. If I'm right, the other five numbers in each line refer to a specific puzzle in one of the books."

"You're a genius, C."

"Yeah, but which puzzles in which books? That's the real riddle."

"And one book, different puzzles. This is giving me a headache already. I can only imagine what it's doing to you."

"I'm the Puzzle Queen, remember?"

She picked up one of the magazines. "Okay, numbers." She turned to the last page. "Ninety-six pages in every issue." She turned to the back where the solutions were printed six to a page. "Seventy-five puzzles plus twelve pages for the solutions and seven pages for ads and publishing data."

"Is it the same for every issue?"

She picked up another one and opened it to the last page. "Ninety-six." Two more yielded the same count.

"That explains why he wanted the same magazine every month." I remembered Boley saying to me on visiting day, "Don't forget my puzzle book, Dunne. I love them *Stellar Crosswords*."

Carlotta wrote "Down/Across" over the sixth column. "Now comes the hard part, figuring out what the other columns mean."

"Any one of them could mean a given month. Do we have a full set?"

Carlotta arranged the magazines in chronological order. July through the following August."

"That'll complicate things a little; we have two duplicate months."

"Look at the bright side," she said. "We just reduced the volume of numbers by sixteen-point-six-seven percent."

"That shrinks the haystack."

Next, we tackled the numbers for months but gave up after two hours, realizing that any of the five columns had the potential to be the right one. "Let's try pages."

Pairs of columns didn't work out either. Two-three, three-four, four-five and five-six all gave numbers that fell into the range of ninety-six pages. Reading the pairs left to right gave the same result. Next, we tried clue numbers. Since none of the puzzles had eighty-two, ninety-two, or ninety-three clues, that eliminated columns two-three. Likewise columns four-five. That narrowed things down by half.

XXXIII

"I'm getting hungry," Carlotta said. "You?"

"Yeah. Let's go get something to eat."

"I'd make us sandwiches, but we cleaned out the fridge before we went to Florida."

"So, get dressed and we'll go The Meatball. They're open for lunch." While Carlotta dressed, I put the crossword magazines back in the box

"Is it the same for every issue?"

and slid it under the coffee table. I folded the papers with our calculations and slid them into the back pocket of my jeans. Carlotta zipped herself into a heavy quilted parka, wrapped a scarf three times around her neck, and pulled a toboggan down over her ears. She still isn't used to Pennsylvania winters. Just to jag her, I didn't bother with a hat or gloves.

The Meatball is the local nickname for Antonini's Restaurant on Cavett Street. It's a three-generation family place that has arguably the best pasta prima vera I've ever tasted. I think the secret family recipe includes anisette, giving their sauce a licorice tang. The place wasn't too busy; the lunch rush was over, and the cold weather didn't help.

I ordered veal parmesan with a side of their homemade spaghetti, and Carlotta had shrimp scampi. Halfway through our meal, Mario, the patriarch came out with a bottle of chianti and two stemware glasses. "Would you like a complimentary glass of wine?" Antonini's doesn't have a liquor license, but they can get away with serving dinner wine as a gift to the patrons.

Carlotta smiled and nodded, and I seconded the motion.

We didn't talk much during the meal, good food precluding conversation. While we were finishing our wine, Carlotta said, "So, Sam, what do we do if we figure all this out?"

"That's a big if." I swirled the last of my chianti in the glass. "I really don't know what to do. We could be good citizens and hand over what we know to the Feds."

"But you don't want to."

"You're right. I don't. Their attitude pisses me off. They think they can just swagger in and push me around."

"That attitude thing goes both ways."

I grinned. "Guilty as charged."

"Well, are you ready to brave the cold again?"

"Ready when you are."

I pulled into a space down the block from our building and when I got out of the car, I saw Blankenship and Tajc's car up the street. As we crossed to the building entrance, I saw the doors open and the agents start down the sidewalk. They weren't hurrying, so I figured I wasn't about to be arrested. They missed the elevator, but by the time we got to the apartment, they were coming through the fire door at the end of the hall.

Nowhere to run, nowhere to hide. I decided to just brazen it out. "Agent Blankenship. Agent Tajc." I nodded to each in turn. "What brings you out on such a cold afternoon?"

"Can the wise-ass, Dunne," Tajc said.

Blankenship pulled a folded paper from his pocket. "We have a warrant to search the premises. So, if you don't want to unlock the door —" I stepped aside and they saw the ragged wood from the break-in.

"You'll kick it in?" I looked pointedly to the door jamb. "You're running second place on that one."

"When did this happen?" Blankenship said.

"A few days ago while we were out of town. The Hanniston PD took the security cam footage if you want to see the perps."

Tajc and Blankenship looked at each other then back at me. "Open the door."

"I never argue with a judge." I unlocked the door, and the agents went in ahead of us. I whispered to Carlotta. "You follow Blankenship, I'll follow Tajc. Have your cell phone ready to take a video if things go wrong."

I stepped over to my desk. "I feel obligated to tell you fellows that I am carrying a firearm, and yes, it is loaded, and yes, I have a permit to carry it." I saw Tajc's hand move inside his coat. "I am now going to open my coat, remove it still in the holster, and set it on the desk." Neither agent moved as I reached under my sweater and unclipped my Beretta from my belt. I held it between thumb and forefinger and set it on the corner of the desk. Blankenship picked it up, dropped the magazine, and jacked the round from the chamber. He put the magazine in his pocket, leaving me one bullet lying beside the pistol, just like Barney Fife. If I wanted to shoot both of them, I'd have to get them to stand single file.

The pistol wasn't the real issue. I gambled that since I gave it up, they felt no need to search me. I was more worried about our notes on the code still in my back pocket.

They stayed together at first, working the living room from end to end. They pulled books from shelves, tossing them on the floor as they went. They threw cushions from the sofa, overturned the recliner, and generally made a mess, probably trying to piss me off. I didn't take the bait. I just stood by as they generally took the place apart. I didn't breathe when Tajc picked up the box with the crossword magazines, but he just turned the box over, spilling them on the floor. Apparently, Weintraub didn't bother to tell them the magazines were part of Boley's legacy. My desk was next. They pulled out every drawer and dumped it on the carpet. Tajc picked up my brass knuckles. "What're these?"

"Paperweight," I said.

He slipped his hand into them and tried them in his open palm. He laughed and threw them back on the desk with a thud. "You need those more than I do."

Blankenship found the envelope with Boley's stuff from Lewisburg. He spread the objects out on the desk and checked them one by one against the inventory written on the front. He looked up and said to Tajc. "It's all here but three guitar picks."

I pointed to the ashtray I used for paper clips. "In there."

Blankenship held each of the copper picks to the light and examined it like he'd find the meaning of life engraved on one of them. From the look on his face, I could see he wasn't pleased.

Next, they split up, Tajc taking the kitchen and Blankenship going into the bedroom. I hung with Tajc. After he clattered through all the pots and pans under the sink, he did a cursory job of going through the cupboards. It was obvious they weren't finding what they wanted. I couldn't hide a guitar in the silverware drawer.

Blankenship came out of the bedroom with the scuffed pickguard in his hand. I'd thrown it in a box of odd and end guitar parts on a shelf in the closet. "Want to explain this?"

"It's a pickguard from one of my old guitars."

"Metal? What is it, aluminum?"

"Good guess. The idea is to cut down signal hum by shielding the wiring inside."

He turned it over in his hands and pointed to the area Snick ground away. "And this?"

I thought fast. "I hot rodded the guitar, put in an active pre-amp, and it didn't quite fit. Had to grind away some of the metal so the guard would screw down flat."

He handed it to me, looking less than convinced.

Tajc came out of the bathroom shaking his head. "Nothing."

"All right, Dunne," Blankenship said. "Where's the guitar?"

"What guitar?"

"Boley Watts' guitar, the one he made in the joint, the one he left you in his will, according to that shyster Weintraub. That guitar."

I made a palms-up gesture. "Not here, fellas."

Tajc started toward me but Blankenship held up a restraining hand. "We know it's not here. Where is it?"

"Well, I gave it to a couple of my friends to look at, pass it around, help me put a price on it. One of them was going to take it to a guitar shop in Pittsburgh to have it appraised for me. I don't know who has it at the moment."

"Miss?"

Carlotta shrugged. "Don't know."

"You know, Dunne, obstructing a Federal investigation carries jail time. Maybe you could build a guitar of your own."

"Can't tell you what I don't know, Agent Blankenship."

He handed me a card. "When you find out where it is, give me a call. Come on, Ralph," Blankenship said to Tajc. He stopped at the threshold and looked back. "And don't take too long to do it." They left, slamming the door. I waited for the ding of the elevator before I said anything. "Well, that was interesting."

"It'll take the rest of the day to put back everything they threw around."

"Tajc looked in every nook and cranny. How about Blankenship?"

"He was more interested in the guitar cases in the closet than my underwear drawer. How much do you think they know?"

"Zip. They're still fishing. They have nothing concrete on me; otherwise, they would've hauled me away in bracelets by now."

I tipped the recliner upright and slumped into it. "One thing's for sure."

"What?"

"They aren't giving up."

"What do you do if they come back with a court order for you to produce the guitar?"

"Then I guess I'll throw in the towel." I sat up. "But in the meantime, we can still try to solve the puzzle."

If Blankenship and Tajc were waiting for me to panic and make a frantic phone call to whoever was holding onto Baby, they were disappointed. Likewise, if they were sitting in their car waiting for me to go somewhere so they could follow me, they were wasting their time.

I pulled our work notes from my back pocket. "Glad I didn't leave these lying around."

Carlotta spread the pages out on the coffee table. "So, we know column six is Across or Down. We need a single column and two pairs that make sense."

"Why don't we just try running one possibility and see what happens?"

"I suppose we could, although it'll take a lot of time to do it that way. Let's be logical and work in descending magnitude."

"Huh?"

"No offense to Boley, but he wasn't exactly James Bond. I don't see him making the code too devious, since it was intended for him to be able to work it out if his memory failed him. The biggest unit would be the month, second is the page, and third is the clue number. Column one for the month means the page and clue columns are either two-three or four-five." Let's try it."

We worked our way through the first four lines left to right and got a nonsense cluster of words: Frog Bevy Circle Destiny. When Carlotta tried line five, she said. "Uh oh."

"What's the matter?"

"The other puzzles are done. He never touched this one."

"So look at the answer key in the back." We did, and it gave us the word Adversary. Line six gave us a finished puzzle and the sixth word, Analog.

"Frog Bevy Circle Destiny Adversary Analog. That makes a lot of sense."

Carlotta frowned. "Write it down. We can always go back and try scrambling the letters. There's a computer app on line that'll do it for us. Let's try door Number Two.

The second line led us to three puzzles that were untouched and the message: Noisome Cats Stet Vehicle Consult Attack.

I wrote it down. "This isn't getting us anywhere."

"Maybe we're going at this the wrong way. When I looked for numbers in the magazine, I was thinking page numbers." She flipped through one of the issues. "One puzzle to a page."

"How else could they print it? If they put two on a page, the print would be so small you'd need a microscope to read it."

"What if columns two-three don't stand for a page number? What if they stand for a puzzle number?"

"They wouldn't jibe one-to-one with the pages; they'd be offset by three or four."

"Let's try this again."

The August issue, puzzle twenty-seven, fifteen down. Carlotta turned to the puzzle in the earlier of the August magazines. "Fifteen down: seven letters meaning missive: letter." She leafed through the later August issue. "Eight letters meaning jointure: union. So it's either missive or union. What's the next one?"

"January, puzzle forty-three, eight across."

Carlotta flipped through the January issue. "Here's forty-three. Eight across: four letters, less than a city: town."

"Uniontown," I said. "That's where Boley and his partners pulled their last bank job."

"Next?"

"September, puzzle thirty-one, twenty-two across."

"Three letters, blank for tat: tit." Carlotta was getting excited now.

"September again, puzzle thirty-one, sixteen down."

"Three letters, cattle call: low."

"June, puzzle forty-one, four down."

"Five letters, beneath: under."

"Last one, May, puzzle thirty-seven six across."

"Eight letters, steam heater."

We looked at each other and said in unison, "Radiator."

"I read off the six words: "Union town tit low under radiator."

"So, what's the tit low reference mean?"

"I don't know, but I bet Google does."

I decided to use my phone to access the Internet. The fact that Blankenship and Tajc didn't take my computer with them told me that they already had online access to monitor it and were just waiting for me to use it. I typed in Union town tit low on my cell phone's browser. For good measure, since Uniontown's a common name, I added Pennsylvania so that I didn't get a hundred hits from anywhere with a license plate. A half dozen websites popped up. I clicked on one and held the phone over for Carlotta to see it. "It's a hotel, C., in Uniontown down the street from the Bank Boley robbed."

Uniontown was about three hours away, and I was ready to jump in the van and head for the Turnpike, but Carlotta talked me out of it.

"Look out the window."

I did and saw that a thick, gauzy snow was falling again.

"You might make it in five hours if you can get over the mountains between here and New Stanton. And what will you do when you get there; tell them you're a plumbing inspector there to check the radiators? I'm as excited as you are, but you have to think this through before you make a move."

She was right, and the longer I watched the snow fall, the less inviting the prospect of a road trip looked. "I agree. No sense jumping in the pool before we see whether there's water in it."

"If we're right, if Boley was right, and the money's there today, it'll still be there tomorrow and next week. We aren't running a race."

"Yeah, but now that I know for sure that the Feds are after Baby, I have to let a few people know. Razor, I'm not so worried about, but I don't want Tajc and Blankenship busting in on Johnny at the store. I don't want him to have trouble because of me. And there's Tanner and those two guys in the beat-up car. Too many doors to watch." I elbowed Carlotta. "Think we should have stayed in Florida?"

"Are you kidding? And miss all this excitement, adventure, and intrigue? No way, love. I feel like I'm living in a novel."

XXXIV

Uniontown. So close and yet so far. I had a real lead on the missing money now, and Carlotta to thank for it. I may have figured out the clues in the crossword books eventually, but by then, I'd be in a nursing home. I had a good idea where the money was stashed, but I needed to narrow it down before I started tearing up the floors in the Titlow. According to their website, the Titlow had four floors, the first taken up by a bar and restaurant. The rooms on the second floor had been recently made over into a bed and breakfast venue, and the upper floors were waiting to be renovated.

The Titlow's website touted the old-time charm of the century-old building, and photographs of two of the rooms showed old cast iron radiators under the tall windows. Okay, I thought, is the money under you, or under you? Or is it somewhere else, or is it even there at all? Did some carpenter or plumber pull up the floorboards in the right room and find the cash? I tended to think that Boley was right; if someone had found the money and spent just one of the sequential bills, the FBI or the Treasury Department would know because of their computer tracking system. It was still there. Or it wasn't. Either way, I had to find out.

I called the number on the website and got Scott Payden, the owner on the phone.

"Mr. Payden? My name is Sam Dunne. I'm a writer and I'm working on a biography of the blues musician Eight-String Watts. I'm wondering if you can help me track down some information."

"Depends." I hate it when people use that word. It usually means if there's something in it for me and I can negotiate it upward. "What do you need to know?"

"Do you remember a bank robbery in Uniontown twenty-two years ago? Right down the street from you, wasn't it?"

"Twenty-two years ago I lived in Manassas, Virginia. I bought this place in '98. I don't know anything about a bank robbery."

"Well, it was the robbery that put Watts behind bars for the rest of his life and got his partners killed. I have reason to believe that Watts and his partners stayed in the Titlow at least one night, maybe more than one before the robbery while they were casing the bank and making their plans. Watts told me that when I interviewed him."

"How can I help you?"

"Do you have your old guest registers? Say, covering 1965?"

"I might. I'd have to look."

Time to bait the hook. "If it turned out that you had a trio of notorious bank robbers staying at your hotel, it would add to the cache of the bed and breakfast: Stay in the same room as…You could put the register with the signature under glass and promo the place as a gangster's hideout."

Silence. Three count. "A book huh? I'll look through the registers and get back to you. What's your phone number?" I gave him my cell number and said, "I'll wait to hear from you. No rush." I didn't want to sound too anxious and make Payden suspicious. In my head, I was screaming, go look you son of a bitch—now! I hung up and went to the kitchen for another cup of coffee. Time to go through my interview notes with Boley. I wanted to set a date range for times when the robbers might have stayed at the Titlow. I really was interested only in the day of the robbery and the day after when the bank robbers were hiding in Uniontown, but to keep Payden from getting wise, I had to make it look as if I was feeling my way in the dark.

Another chore I had to do was go online and search the newspaper database for accounts of the robbery. When I showed up at the Titlow, I wanted Payden to see a file folder stuffed with clippings. If I was going to play the role of researcher, I'd better make it look good.

One of the privileges I enjoy as an adjunct instructor at HACC is unlimited access to their library's research databases. Two hours at the library terminal gave me dozens of articles from six newspapers including the Uniontown *Herald-Standard*. I printed them out—for free, another perk for faculty members—and came back to the apartment with a thick file of research.

Carlotta and I read through the articles, but none of them seemed to offer anything I didn't know anyway. Carlotta dog-eared a few of the photocopies and marked a few passages in some of them with a yellow highlighter. "If this guy—Payden? That's his name?—picks up any of these papers while you're working there, you don't want them to look like you haven't even read them yourself."

"Good point." That's my girl.

I have patience, but not nearly enough. I was climbing the walls by the time I finally heard from Payden the day after I called him. "Mr. Dunne? Scott Payden. I found two registers that between them cover 1995."

"Great. Would it be inconvenient for me to come there and go through them?" I was going to ask if he'd mail them to me, but I wanted to see the place firsthand.

"I doubt it. When would you like to come?"

"Some time in the next two or three days. I'll call in advance."

"Where are you coming from?"

"Hanniston; middle of the state."

"You mean the Commonwealth."

"Huh?"

"One thing Pennsylvania and Virginia have in common, if you'll pardon the pun, is that neither is a state. Both are Commonwealths."

"Got it."

"So, will you be needing a room?"

"Yeah, because I don't know what the weather's going to do."

"All right. When you decide on a date, give me a call and I'll set it up for you."

I hadn't thought about it to that point, but if I stayed the night, I might get a chance to look around the place in the wee hours. "I'll call you back sometime tomorrow." And there we left it.

When Carlotta came home from work, she said, "Well?"

"Road trip."

"You're taking me with you, of course."

"Wouldn't be the same without you."

"I want to be there when you find the money."

I hugged her. "Considering you solved the puzzle, it's only fair."

She shrugged out of her coat and started unbuttoning her uniform. "I'm going to ditch the rayon and put on something warmer. I have to go to the grocery to buy something to cook tonight." She disappeared into the bedroom and came back out five minutes later in jeans and a sweater. "Any special requests?"

"We haven't had shrimp for while. How about that?"

"That sounds reasonable." She pulled on her parka. "God, I hate to go out in that cold and snow again."

"Do you want me to go?"

She shook her head. "No, you stay here. If I send you to Safeway for a pound of butter, you'll come back with Cheetos, pork rinds, a pack of Twinkies, and a half gallon of Breyer's ice cream."

"The four basic food groups."

"We weigh enough already." She tugged her toboggan over her ears. "See you in a half hour."

I did what I usually do when I'm stressed. I took my old Martin acoustic off the wall and played for a while. I did a few finger-picking rags and a couple of blues songs, and before I knew it, thirty minutes had passed, and Carlotta hadn't come back. I gave it another fifteen minutes and called her cell phone. My call went to voice mail. "Hey, C. are you stuck in the snow? Give me a call and I'll send out the Mounties." My words were jovial, but my tone didn't quite match. After another fifteen minutes, I put on my coat.

The Safeway is in a strip mall about two miles from the apartment, and I made better than average time jogging through the snow. The parking lot wasn't crowded, and I spotted the Caravan right away. Okay, I thought, she's still in the store; probably ran into someone she knows and stopped to talk for a while. Feeling foolish, I walked around the driver's side of the van and I saw her purse lying in the snow. I picked it up and rummaged through it. Her wallet and phone were still in it.

I ran into the store and must have looked like a lunatic running from aisle to aisle clutching a purse in both hands. She wasn't there. A store manager came up to me, keeping his distance in case I might snap out and tear off his head. "Uh, sir, is there a problem?"

I didn't answer. I ran past him out of the store and jumped into the van, digging in my pocket for the keys. I was halfway back to the apartment when my cell phone rang. The Caller ID showed an unfamiliar number.

"Hello."

Nobody spoke for about ten seconds then a husky voice said, "You got somethin' we want. We got somethin' you want. Let's make a deal." By the voice and dialect, I figured it was one of the guys in the Buick. The voice was phlegmy and a little ragged, but confident; not the bravado of some young punk, but the mature self-assurance of an older, experienced man.

"Where is she?"

"She safe and warm right now. Got a nice tattoo on her shoulder. Virgo." He chuckled. "I don't guess she's a virgin by now, but if you jack us around and make us wait, I guarantee she won't be one when you get here."

I knew threats and pleas would only stoke his sense of control. "What do you want?"

"You have to ask? Boley Watts' guitar." He pronounced it "git-tar."

"I don't have it with me. I'll have to go get it."

"You do that. I'll call you back in an hour. You call the cops or pull any clever shit, you know what'll happen."

"How do I know you really have her? Let me talk to her."

In a second, I heard Carlotta's voice. "Sam."

"Are you all right, C.? Have they hurt you?"

Her voice was slow and a little slurred. Drugged. "No. No one's hurt me. But I'm cold. So cold. Come get me, Sam."

"I will, babe, I —"

"That's enough, Dunne. Go get the guitar. You got one hour, and then Lavalle gonna start entertainin' your woman." The line went dead.

I didn't wait to get back to the apartment to use Razor's emergency number.

"What's up?"

"It's Sam. I need Baby right now."

"Okay, tell me what happened."

I gave him a quick account of Carlotta's disappearance and the phone call from the kidnappers. "I'll go with you."

"No, they said I have to bring the guitar alone and don't call the cops."

"I agree with that last part. Trust me, Sam. They won't even know I'm there—'til it's too late. I'll meet you at your place in half an hour."

If the hour I waited for Carlotta seemed like a long time, the half hour I waited for Razor seemed double. I checked the clip in the Beretta three times. I had a shot of Jack Daniels to calm me down, and by the time my cell phone rang, I was as calm as I was going to get. "Yeah?"

It was Razor. "I'm down front. I put the guitar in the back of your van. I did a little modification to it."

"What did you do, hide a shotgun in the wiring cavity?"

"No, but if you can get the pickguard off, watch your fingers. I ground a good sharp edge on one side."

"Oh man," I sighed.

"It won't come to that if I get my way. Hold it together, man. When you get the call, come down and I'll follow you."

"Maybe you ought to come up."

"Maybe one of them's watching your building. Besides, depending on what might happen, I really don't want my face on a security camera. Don't worry, I'll be behind you. You may not see me, but I'll be there."

I had a shot of Jack Daniels to calm me down.

He rang off, and the next half hour passed even more slowly as I waited for the kidnappers to call and my imagination painted nightmare scenes of what they were doing to Carlotta. I didn't give a damn about the money now. I was ready to do whatever it took to get her back safe.

XXXV

My phone erupted with its ring tone, the guitar solo from Funkadelic's "Maggot Brain," and I answered it in less than a second.

"Dunne?" It was the same man who'd called earlier.

"Yeah, it's Dunne."

"Get in your car and start driving. Head out of town on Route twenty-seven. "I'll call you back in a few minutes. And Dunne?" There was some dead air space. "No cops, no tricks. Do what you're told, and the lady won't get hurt. Piss around and —" The line went dead.

I called Razor. He answered without speaking.

"It's on."

"Right behind you."

As I climbed in the van, the thought occurred to me that all this time I'd seen only two of them. If they both were holding Carlotta captive, they didn't have anyone to watch my building or to follow me to know I was doing what I was told. But what if they had another accomplice I hadn't seen? For that matter, what if they were working for Tanner? I decided that if that was the case, if any harm came to Carlotta, I wouldn't send Jerome. I'd hunt Tanner down and kill him myself, no matter what the consequences.

I was a mile out of Hanniston and didn't see any lights in my mirror. The snow was falling more heavily now, and the only lights I saw on the road had a yellow spinner overhead. They were the headlights of a Penn DOT truck plowing the opposite lane.

My phone rang. "Yeah."

"Okay, Dunne." Different voice, same accent.

"Is this Lavalle?"

"Knowin' names don't do you no good, Dunne." Turn your car around and drive back toward town." Headlights came on fifty yards behind me. "When you get behind that plow truck, follow it to I-80, and head south."

"How far?"

"Don't hang up. Just set the phone on the seat. I'll tell you when to get off the Interstate. In the meantime, just shut up and drive."

They were better than I gave them credit. They had me drive the wrong direction far enough to lose a tail, if I had one, and now Lavalle was tying up my phone and had an ear in my van in case I managed to bring somebody with me. I decided that Razor wasn't riding to the rescue. I had to manage this on my own.

I got on 80 South and the plow truck kept going. The lights behind me never wavered an inch. It was as if an invisible chain linked my van and the Buick. I put my phone on speaker and laid it on the passenger seat so I could drive with both hands. 80 had been plowed once, but the snow continued to fall. I saw the light bar of a State Police car behind us and coming fast. Could I signal him? What would happen if I did? Before I could think about it anymore, he whipped past me in a swirling cloud of snow. I was going forty, he was going eighty. The flashing lights melted into the blizzard.

The voice buzzed in my phone. "Half a mile, you see the exit for Biggs Road. Take it and go left at the intersection. I saw the highway sign for the exit and just behind it I saw something else, the tall lighted sign for a Motel 6.

I turned as instructed and Lavalle said, "Okay, Dunne. Pull in to the parking lot at the Six. You see two spaces past the white pickup truck. Pull in the one to the right. I wanted to tell him that all three pickup trucks were white from the snow, but I didn't. Only one had two spaces beside it. I pulled into the right-hand space, and the Buick slid in beside me.

Before I could shut off the van, Lavalle was out the passenger door and standing with an old blue steel revolver pointed at me through the window. The thought crossed my mind that I could maybe slam him with the door of the van, but even if I got him on the ground and got his gun away from him, I still wouldn't know which of the rooms had Carlotta in it. I put my hands up at shoulder level and he opened the door with his free hand.

"Okay, Dunne. Out. Slow and easy. Leave the phone on the seat."

I sidled out of the driver's seat and Lavalle said, "Up against the van." He patted me down and found the Beretta, but I expected he would. He put it in his pocket. "Where's the guitar?"

"On the floor behind the front seats."

"You open that door real slow and take it out."

I did what he told me and he pushed his pistol into my back a little harder than I thought necessary and said. "Start walkin' Dunne. Room one-twenty-three."

Now I knew which room. If I had the chance, I'd take Lavalle down, but the gun in my back told me that was a slim chance. Okay, Razor, I thought, now would be a good time to show up. I wanted to turn my head, look around and see whether he was able to follow me, but I couldn't risk giving him away if he did. As I walked past the ground-floor rooms, I caught glimpses of the parking lot reflected in the big plate-glass windows. The snow-covered lot glowed orange in the arc lights and was as still as a graveyard. If there were security cams in the lot, the blizzard made them useless. Everyone was in for the night. I strained my ears but heard nothing other than the soft hiss of falling snow.

We reached the door of 123 and Lavalle reached around me to rap on it. Two knocks then three. I heard the click of the dead bolt and the ratchet of the safety chain. From the other side of the door I heard the loud canned laughter of a sitcom on the television. The door swung inward, and Lavalle prodded me into the room.

Two double beds with a nightstand between them, low-boy dresser under a mirror, and two chairs at a table littered with fast food wrappers and empty beer cans. Carlotta was tied, naked, to one of the chairs, her clothes in a pile on the floor beside it. I guess they figured that if she got untied and escaped somehow, she wouldn't get far in the snow. Her head lolled onto her left shoulder. At least she wasn't awake and aware of what was going down.

"Put it down, Dunne," Lavalle said. "On the dresser."

I laid the box down and in the mirror; I got a good look at Carlotta's abductors. Lavalle looked to be somewhere between fifty and fifty-five, his close-cropped hair threaded with gray. He was tall and rangy, his overcoat hanging on him like a scarecrow's. He was still pointing the revolver at me. His companion was dressed in a shiny blue running suit with the Nike swoosh on the chest and white high-top Chuck Taylors. His hair was longer; not quite an Afro, and he wore heavy framed glasses. He was younger than Lavalle, and he looked like he was in good shape. A set of parallel tracks from Carlotta's fingernails ran down his right cheek.

"Open it up," Lavalle said, "and no tricks." I looked in the mirror again and saw that Lavalle's partner, sitting in the other chair, had pulled a pistol of his own and was casually pointing it at Carlotta.

"Which one of you plays guitar?"

No answer.

"You're going to a lot of trouble for an instrument you can't even play."

No answer.

Razor had tied the angular cardboard box with two strands of twine. I fumbled at the tight knots with my fingers, and Lavalle said, "Shit. Middy, gimme your knife." Using names; not a good sign. I got the impression they didn't plan on letting us walk out alive.

Middy unzipped the pocket of his running pants and took out a long, thin folding knife with pearl handles. Lavalle cut the twine and said, "Open the box, Dunne."

I took off the lid and found Baby wrapped in a beach towel. "Now what?"

"Take it out of the box and lay it on the dresser."

I did, and I turned to face Lavalle and Middy. "Okay, guys, I get it. You want the money from the bank job, right?"

"It belongs to us," Middy said.

"Belongs to you?"

"It's our inheritance," Lavalle said. "You don't get it do you Dunne? Middy here's Rufus Small's grandson. My daddy was Boley Watts."

I looked more closely at Lavalle and could see the resemblance. "Boley told me he didn't have any children."

Lavalle snorted. "He knocked up my momma one night in Memphis, and she never saw him again. But she told me all about him, played his records all day long 'til she died, and she cried when he went to jail. But I didn't." Lavalle's voice took on a hard edge. "I hated that bastard with all my heart, and when I read he died and that money was still out there, I figured it belonged to me and Middy. I started lookin' and people I knew in the Joint told me about the guitar."

"You won't find a hundred grand in the guitar," I said. "No room."

"Maybe I'll find where they hid it."

"No need to tear up the guitar. Got a screwdriver?"

Middy went out to the car and came back with an odd-and-end collection of tools from the Buick's trunk. One of them was a Phillips the right size. "There was a set of numbers written inside the cavity with the wiring. Under here." I tapped the aluminum with a fingernail. "Maybe that's what you want."

"Show us."

I took out the screws and slid the pickguard away from the cavity. I could feel the sharp edge Razor had ground in the aluminum. "Right in there." I pointed at the colored wires.

Lavalle did exactly what I wanted him to do. In his excitement, he let his gun hand down and leaned over Baby, craning his neck to look inside.

"I don't see—"

I had one chance and I took it. I swung around and slashed across Lavalle's windpipe with the sharpened aluminum. His eyes bulged with surprise and he dropped his gun to clutch at his spurting throat. Middy rose from his chair, swinging his pistol around at me, but by that time, I had Baby by the neck and swung her like a Louisville Slugger, catching him on the side of his head. Middy's gun went off, but the bullet went wide. I heard the mirror shatter behind me.

Middy was on the floor now, and I cracked his head a few more times, maybe a dozen, to make sure he wasn't getting up again. I shut off the television. I was lucky it was up so loud; it probably covered the noise of the gunshot for people in the rooms on either side. In the silence that followed, I heard the quiet clicking of the lock. Someone else was coming to the party. I looked to the door and saw that when Middy came back in with the tools, he didn't throw the deadbolt or put on the chain.

I scooped up Lavalle's revolver and rolled behind one of the beds as the door swung open. No one was there.

"Sam?" It was Razor, and I came the closest to crying since I was nine years old.

"Yeah. It's clear." I sagged onto the floor.

Razor came into the room, a Glock in his hand. He shut the door and locked it. "Damn. I guess you didn't need me after all," he said, looking around the room at the carnage.

I stood up and the room spun. I've killed people before, but there's a difference between shooting someone with a pistol and slashing a man's throat or pounding his head to pulp. "Carlotta —"

"She's okay, Sam. Let's get her untied and get out of here."

I used Middy's knife to cut the ropes and Razor and I lifted her onto the bed. She didn't stir, but her breathing was steady. I pulled her clothes on her the best I could and carried her out to the van where I laid her on the back seat. I went back into the room and saw Razor wiping things with a towel from the bathroom. He reached into his pocket and pulled out a handful of bindles. "I was going to spread these around to make it look like a drug deal gone bad, but I don't think the cops would buy a guy with a slit throat beating the other guy to death, especially if we take the murder weapon with us."

"I have an idea. Let me get my phone out of the car."

I called Cotton, hoping he wasn't playing a gig.

"Yo, Sam."

"Cotton, can you reach our friend Mr. Settles? I need to talk with him."

Tiny Settles, the crime lord of Hanniston's black community owed me big for clearing his nephew of a murder rap a few years before. If anyone could clean up the mess in room one-twenty-three, he could. In ten minutes, one of Tiny's men called me back, and plans were made to dispose of Lavalle and Middy.

"What did you touch in here?" Razor looked around the room for anything that might belong to Carlotta or me.

"Just the screwdriver and the knife."

Razor pocketed them. "Put the guitar back in the box and let's go."

I almost closed the door behind me when I remembered Lavalle had taken my Beretta. I didn't have any qualms about rifling the pockets of a dead man, especially one who was going to kill me anyway.

"I'll follow you back," Razor said, "at a discreet distance." He walked away with Baby under one arm. I never did see his car.

Carlotta didn't wake up the whole ride back, and when I parked in front of our building, I had to shake her a few times to get a drowsy response. Her eyes opened and she said sleepily, "Sam?"

"Yeah, C. It's me. Come on, we're home. We have to get you inside." I lifted her out of the van and set her on a pair of unsteady feet. I walked down the sidewalk with an arm around her, holding her up by the waist. I fumbled my keys out of my pocket and opened the door, almost carrying her inside with me. I lucked out. Nobody in the foyer. I rang for the elevator. I probably could have carried Carlotta up the stairs, but I wasn't in such good shape myself at the moment.

The doors slid open and Marty Fillburn from the third floor stepped out in a winter coat and earmuffs. "Hi, Sam, Carlotta." He cocked his head and peered at her face. "Is she okay?"

I put on my best game face and said, "Yeah, just had one too many. Taking her home to bed."

He laughed. "She'll feel that in the morning."

I laughed along with him. "Well, be careful if you're driving. The roads are bad."

He shook his head. "Just going to the Quick Mart for cigarettes. You guys need anything?"

What I need, I thought is for you to shut up and walk away. "No, we're good. See you later. Marty," I breathed a sigh of relief when the elevator doors finally closed. I breathed a bigger one when we were back in the apartment.

I got Carlotta out of her coat, laid her fully dressed on the bed, and covered her with a blanket. I was leaving the room when she said, "Sam? What happened? I can't remember."

All I could think was thank God. I couldn't imagine what would come of her seeing me kill one man, let alone two. I was grateful that she missed the show.

I lay down beside her and put a protective arm around her waist. I kissed her cheek and said, "It's okay, babe. Everything's all right."

If only that were true.

XXXVI

The next morning, I let Carlotta sleep. I called Dora's and told her boss she wasn't feeling well. He wasn't happy about being short-handed, but he wasn't going to fire her, either. I was making coffee when I heard her cry out from the bedroom. I ran in and found her sitting bolt upright, eyes wide, fists curled in the blanket.

I held her. She was shaking and started to cry. "Sam, those men, they grabbed me. I tried to fight them, but they were too strong. One of them stuck a needle in me, they threw me in a car, and I don't remember what happened after that."

"It's okay," I said, holding her tighter. "You're okay, and I'm okay."

"But those men, what if —"

I held her by the shoulders and looked her in the eyes. "They won't bother you again."

Her eyes widened. "Sam, what did you do?"

I decided not to lie. "I killed them both."

She took a long breath and let it out. "Oh God, Sam, the police —"

"There won't be any police. I saw to that. If we just keep our heads, we'll walk away from this. It's over."

"It was about the bank money, wasn't it?"

In for a penny. "Yeah. That's what they were after ."

"Then it isn't over 'til somebody finds it."

"I guess not."

She stared at the floor for a minute then raised her chin. "Then let's make sure it's us."

One more reason to love her.

XXXVII

I watched the local morning news from end to end but didn't hear a word about a dual murder in a Motel 6. Promising, but the day was young. Later that morning I called Scott Payden at the Titlow and told him I'd like to come the next day to look at the registers and stay overnight.

"You're in luck," Payden said. "I have one room left. There's some sort of social services confab going on in town this week, but I had a cancellation. I'll reserve it for you. Are you coming alone?"

"No," I said, smiling at Carlotta, "there'll be two of us."

"Good enough. When do you think you might arrive?"

"Unless it snows again, the trip will be about four hours tops. I'd say two in the afternoon."

I thumbed off my phone. "Well, that's one item down. Now to figure out how to get away without being followed by Blankenship and Tajc, if they're even still in town."

"What about that Tanner guy, the private eye?"

"I don't know what his status is. Maybe Kearny can tell me."

I punched Kearny's desk number into the land line phone. I was lucky; he was in.

"Kearny, it's Sam Dunne."

"Well, I guess you're breathing easier."

"Why's that?"

"Your pals from the Bureau got called away on something more urgent than a twenty-two-year-old bank robbery. I heard the Chief say something about it."

"That's good news, but that's not why I called."

"Oh yeah?"

"I was hoping you could tell me what happened with that guy who got nabbed for passing counterfeit twenties."

"The private eye? I suppose I could ask around, but I have to ask you why."

"Curiosity."

"Don't shit me, Sam. This is Mike Kearny you're talking to. You never do anything for one reason only. And by the way, I don't recall the news reports saying the bills were twenties."

"That's what I heard."

"Uh-huh. I bet."

"Don't I get any favors for saving your life?"

He laughed. "How many times are you cashing that check? All right, Sam. I'll ask downstairs and call you back."

"Good news," I told Carlotta. "Blankenship and Tajc left town. Kearny'll call back when he finds out about Tanner."

"I'm glad they're gone, but at the same time I wish they'd been around to follow you last night."

"And come into the room with guns blazing. We might all have been killed."

"I suppose you're right." She shuddered, "but I get cold thinking about it."

"Then maybe you shouldn't."

The phone rang. It was Kearny.

"The counterfeiter—Tanner?—was bailed out yesterday afternoon."

"One of the bondsmen pay the tab?"

"Nope, a civilian, man named Richard Knight. Ten grand cash knocked down from twenty. The guys on duty said Knight was a vest with some clout with the feds."

Tanner's mysterious client, I thought. "So he's out of the cage, huh?"

"Free for the moment, but he can't leave the county without permission. Anything else I can do for you? Check your stocks on the Dow Jones Index?"

"No, you told me what I need to know."

"We serve and protect." He hung up and left me staring at the handset.

Serve, yes, but I couldn't expect any protection from the law. If I went to the cops for help now, I'd have too many questions to answer, and too many people to drag down with me. I had to manage this on my own dime.

"Tanner's out of jail."

"Damn."

"I just have to assume he's behind me every step of the way. I have to figure out how we can get out of town without him following us or better yet, even knowing we're gone."

"Could you borrow a car? How about Razor's?"

I laughed. "If Razor loaned me a car, I'd probably get about ten miles before some state trooper pulled me over because it's on the hot list."

"What if somebody drives the van in the wrong direction and we go in another car?"

"That might work. Let's think about it. In the meantime, I need to look something up."

The name Richard Knight rang a bell when Kearny said it. I started skimming through my file of news articles about the bank robberies and found him. When Boley and his partners robbed the First National Bank of Uniontown, Richard M. Knight was the bank's Vice-President.

XXXVIII

I spent the next four hours watching the street outside my building. The same three cars were there consistently, but two of them stayed in the same spot. I figured Tanner was in the third car, a gray Dodge charger made nondescript by a coating of frozen slush and road salt. It periodically drove away only to show up again in another parking place down the street a few minutes later. Another hint was that the Charger was the only car of the three with the snow cleaned off the windshield.

That told me one other important thing: Tanner was working alone. For some reason, Knight bailed him out of jail instead of simply getting another PI from his agency. Whatever Tanner was doing for Knight, Knight didn't want it spread around. Like Benjamin Franklin once wrote, three can keep a secret if two of them are dead.

I texted Johnny Malone and told him what I wanted to do. The plan wasn't exactly simple, but it wasn't a major operation either. Carlotta would go to work as usual and take the Caravan with her. She'd leave it in the gravel lot beside Dora's. I'd walk to Malone's carrying a guitar case with an old Gretsch solid body in it. If I was right about Tanner's surveillance, he'd follow me. I was hoping he'd do it on foot.

I would stop at a pay phone and set the case behind me on the ground. If I was lucky, Tanner would grab it and run and while I was busy with the phone. He'd take off with the case, I'd run the other way to Dora's, and Carlotta and I would head for the highway before he could get to his car. Bye-bye, Tanner.

Plan B was a little trickier. If Tanner didn't snatch what he thought was Baby, he'd follow me to Malone's. I'd go inside and set the case on the counter in full view of the street and open the lid as if I were showing Johnny and Nick the guitar inside. They would react as if I'd showed them the Shroud of Turin, and Johnny and I would take it to the back room. I'd go out the basement door and take the alleys to Dora's while Tanner spun his wheels on the street outside.

Either way, it was still a gamble, but I was willing to roll the dice. I realized that if I found the bank money, I'd have to give it up. Sure, I could try to launder it, but I couldn't spend more than twenty dollars of it at a time without having the Feds knocking on my door and wondering whether my musical career had suddenly taken off. They start looking into my life, and maybe the Motel 6 comes into play.

Looking back, if I had any sense, I would have just called the number on Blankenship's card and told him what I knew. I can't say that exactly. I had plenty of sense; it just got eclipsed by the situation. I was into this so deep that I couldn't back out. I had to keep on pushing 'til I came out the other side.

That night, Carlotta and I lay in bed, but I don't think either one of us slept an hour. When her alarm went off at five, we were both wide awake and running on adrenaline.

When she left, Carlotta took my face in both her hands and said, "Here goes, lover. Make it work."

"Walk in the park."

We both knew better.

I stood in the dark in my living room and pulled back the curtain. I saw Carlotta get in the van and drive away. The Charger pulled away from the curb thirty seconds later, lights off.

My cell phone rang. Carlotta. "Okay, Sam, I'm on my way."

"The Charger's behind you, no headlights. Don't hang up 'til you get into Dora's."

"Okay, but I'm going to put the phone on speaker and set it on the seat. I need both hands on the wheel. The streets are icy. Too bad this heap doesn't have Bluetooth."

"If we find the money, I'll buy a new one," I joked. She didn't laugh. I heard the thump of the phone on the seat.

"Headlights behind me." Her voice sounded far away.

"Where are you?"

"Two blocks from Dora's."

"Take it slow and park under the lights. I don't think he'll try anything with you, but you never know."

"I'll keep my hand on my mace."

Neither of us spoke for a couple of minutes, and then she said, "I'm in the lot." Her voice got louder once she picked up the phone. "I'm going inside. The phone will be in my pocket; you should be able to hear if anything happens."

I held my breath waiting, and finally let it out when I heard the bustle of the diner in the background. "I'm in."

"All right. Keep your phone handy, because when I move, it'll be quick."

"Be careful, Sam."

"Always am."

"No, you aren't. Make an effort." She hung up.

XXXIX

I needed sleep, so I set the alarm on the nightstand for eight o'clock, stretched out on the bed in my clothes, and dozed in and out 'til I looked at the clock and it said 7:57. I shut off the alarm. Almost time to make things happen. I went to the window and looked out. The gray Charger wasn't in my field of vision, but I knew it had to be out there.

At nine, I called Malone's. Johnny answered, and I said, "Okay to bring the guitar in?"

"Yeah, Sam. I'll be here."

I hung up the phone, clipped the Beretta onto my belt, put on my coat, and started the wheels turning.

On the street, the sky was pearl gray. The air was sharp and clear as it often is after a heavy snow cleans all the pollution and crap out of the atmosphere. I left the building and started down the street. I had the guitar in one hand, and in the other, a small makeup mirror from Carlotta's purse. I put my hand up to my face to adjust my sunglasses and looked at the street behind me. Someone was getting out of a car half a block behind; tall, rangy, wearing a leather jacket but still sporting a fedora. Tanner.

Shoveled snow turned the sidewalks into trenches. Hanniston was back to work, but the winter mess put it in low gear. Rock salt crunched under my feet. The closest pay phone to the apartment was outside the convenience store. They're slowly vanishing as more people buy cell phones. Something Darwinian about that.

I set the guitar on the sidewalk and picked up the handset. The earpiece was cold enough to be painful. I punched in a fake number and turned my back to the guitar. I could see the reflection of the sidewalk behind me in the display window of a store across the street.

I watched and waited. People passed by in both directions, but no one grabbed the guitar. I hung up the phone. I knew that Tanner was back there someplace. Time for Plan B.

Someone was getting out of a car half a block behind... Tanner.

I didn't catch a glimpse of Tanner the rest of the way to Malone's, and I wasn't surprised. After all, he was a private eye doing what private eyes do best. When I got to Malone's Nick was out front throwing salt on the sidewalk.

"Sam the man," he said. "What you got there?"

"Something special, Nick. Come on and take a look." I said that a little louder than usual, hoping Tanner would hear it.

Nick and I went inside, and through the display window I spotted Tanner standing in a doorway across the street. I set the case on the counter and Johnny came out of the back room. I opened the lid as planned and Johnny and Nick put on the show. I hoped Tanner could see it all.

Johnny and I took the guitar back to his workshop while Nick stayed out front at the counter, ready to buzz Johnny on the intercom if Tanner came in.

"Okay, Sam, the bar's off the door downstairs. Good luck."

"Thanks, Johnny." I slipped down the basement stairs and through the darkened store room. I opened the outside door and stuck out my head. Nobody in sight. I closed the door behind me and took off at a quick trot for Dora's. I thumbed the phone and called Carlotta. "On my way."

"I'll be in the car."

I found out later that Tanner came into the store, looked every direction and headed to the back over Nick's protests. He barged into Johnny's workshop in spite of the sign that said Employees Only to find Johnny in a shooter's stance with his .38 aimed at Tanner's head.

Johnny cocked the hammer and said, "Can I help you?"

Tanner might have been a problem, but out on bail, the last thing he could risk was a run-in involving the cops. He turned around and ran back out the way he came.

XL

I made it to Dora's in minutes and Carlotta had the car warmed up. I slid into the passenger seat and said. "Let's motor."

We got on the Interstate and covered the distance to the Turnpike in less than ten minutes. The Caravan breezed through the toll booth with the E-Z Pass and once we got on the west ramp, I figured Tanner could never follow us because he wouldn't know which direction we went.

"I'm betting you didn't eat breakfast," Carlotta said.

"Guilty as charged."

"There's a bag behind the seat. I had Betty make some sandwiches and there's a large coffee to go in the cup holder."

One more reason to love her.

After I ate, I took over driving and found the wind on the Turnpike was brutal. It swept across the flat farmland in the middle of the state like a like a big open palm pushing against the side of the van. I was glad in one way to get into the foothills and finally the Allegheny Mountains; the mountains blocked most of the wind, but once we hit the foothills, the snow was falling again. The four tunnels through the mountains had the only non-white surface on the pavement.

I got behind a Penn DOT truck and settled in at fifty miles an hour, letting the State clear my path for me. My tax dollars at work. I called Payden and let him know we'd be arriving late and told him to hold our room.

I wasn't happy about the slow pace, but Carlotta put it in perspective: we'd get there late, but we'd get there. Unlike one clown who zipped past me in a red Jeep Cherokee at about seventy-five. People forget that just because you can get moving better with four-wheel drive, you can't brake or steer any better. A half-hour after he passed me, I passed him. The Jeep was upside down in the median.

Uniontown was about forty-five minutes from the Turnpike, and we made it there just before dark. I found the Titlow at the west end of a one-way Main Street.

From the outside, the Titlow looked like it had been dropped onto the modernized city street from a century before. The building was red brick, darkened by half a century of coke oven soot before the mines and the mills shut down during the Depression.

We walked through an old revolving door set between leaded glass panes and felt as if we were stepping into the turn of the twentieth century. Instead of a foyer, we found a long room with a marble floor and a stone hearth with a fire blazing in the grate. Comfortable armchairs and low tables were arranged in a half moon around the fireplace, occupied by a handful of people with drinks.

I asked a waitress where to find the registration desk and she told me to go through the tavern. The tavern reminded me a little of Casey's, full of old oak and polished brass. I almost expected to see spittoons on the black and white hex-tiled floor. The bar was enormous, and behind it, mirrors doubled the ranks of bottles lined up in front of them.

Carlotta was delighted with the place. "Wow, Sam, this place is beautiful."

"Thank you."

We turned and found ourselves facing a man in his late thirties whom I'd describe as a consummate yuppie. His perfect smile cost somebody at least thirty grand. Not one blond hair was out of place in his perfectly trimmed mustache or on top of his head. I don't know fashion trademarks, but I know expensive when I see it.

"I'm Scott Paden," he said, holding out his hand for a shake. "I'm the owner. I haven't met you folks before, have I?"

"Sam Dunne," I said, taking the offered hand. "We talked on the phone."

Payden gave my hand a professional three pumps. "And the lady?"

"This is Carlotta Bell."

"How was your drive in?"

"Snowy; heavy over the mountains. Typical Pennsylvania February."

"Well, we're glad to have you here."

A petite Barbie Doll blond appeared at Payden's side. "This my wife Julie. Honey, this is Sam Dunne, the writer I told you about, and this is Carlotta Bell."

She must have gone to the same dentist. "Scott said you're writing a book. That's exciting." She showed polite interest, so I gave her a polite answer.

"I hope a major publisher agrees with you."

"Have you brought in your bags?

"No, they're out in the van."

"I'll help you with them. Are you parked in the lot?"

"No, I'm out front on the street."

"We have the lot across the alley. Pull around and I'll meet you there."

Payden came out in a Land's End parka as I was taking our things out of the car. "I'll take the overnight bag," I said. "You can get the box." I didn't want him handling my bag and wondering why it was so heavy. What would a writer need with a flooring bar, a chisel, and a monkey wrench?

He picked up the box of files. "A lot of research, I see."

"You have to dig to find the diamonds."

"I searched Amazon but I didn't find anything you'd written."

"This is my first book. I'm a professional musician, and a singer-song-writer. I moonlight as an English prof."

Payden nodded. "I saw a Sam Dunne mentioned in the blurb for a book called *Dead Man's Melody* by a woman—."

"Wendy Conn."

"Yeah, that's her." He had better teeth and hair than I did, but I could kick his ass in a grammar competition. He didn't bring up Danny Barton. "We've put you in Room two-eight. I hope you'll like it."

"I'm sure it'll be fine." We went in a side entrance and I saw a registration counter styled the same way as the bar. A faded red-on-white sign hung on the wall beside it that said "Rooms $2 a night." Behind the counter were a set of pigeon holes and a hookboard with old-fashioned skeleton keys attached to numbered fobs.

"Those are the old original keys," Payden said, setting the file box on the counter beside a brass call bell." The former owners replaced the locks thirty years or so ago. The old keys lend to the ambiance. You'd be surprised how many people take selfies in front of the desk."

Carlotta came out of the tavern chatting with Julie like they were old buddies. "Sam, they're having blackened catfish as tonight's dinner special."

"Sounds great." I turned to Payden. "Could somebody show us the way to the room?"

"I'll take you," Julie said. "Right up the stairs. Just follow me."

We climbed the stairs to the second floor, and I noticed the stairwell leading upward was hung with sheet plastic. "We're renovating the third floor now so that we have the rooms available for the summer."

"Big job?"

"A little plastering, paint all around, that sort of thing. Here's your room."

The room was a little bigger than the room at home where I grew up. It had a double bed with a granny-square quilt, a faux Tiffany lamp on a nightstand, and one ladder-backed chair. No closet. A row of brass hooks lined the wall on one side. Under the window a cast iron radiator was ticking away making the room a little short of cozy.

"Ooh, it's chilly in here." Julie hugged herself. "I'll turn up the heat. She bent over the radiator and fiddled with the valve. "The bathroom's down at the end of the hall," she said over her shoulder.

The radiator started hissing and replaced the ticking with an occasional clank. "That'll do it," Julie said. "If you need anything before dinner, push that button." She pointed to what looked like a doorbell buzzer. "We don't have phones in the rooms yet, but no one seems to mind much. Everybody has a cell phone these days."

"You could ask Scott if I could look at the registers before supper."

Julie nodded. "Will do."

Carlotta and I waited a full minute before we spoke.

"Well, here's hoping," I said.

"Don't wish too hard, Sam. You know what happens."

Fifteen minutes later, Payden was at the door with the registers, nine-by-twelve clothbound books with red leather corners. "Here they are. I hope you find something useful. You don't have much room to work up here. Would you like to use my office?"

"I'll be all right, but thanks. How late do you serve supper?"

"We serve supper 'til nine."

What I needed to see would take me all of about five minutes, but I had to make it look as if I were involved in a long, tedious search. "We'll be sure to make it before then."

I knew the date of the robbery, and according to Boley the robbers hid in the Titlow for at least two days before the shootout. The news reports put the robbery at two o'clock on June twenty-third and the shootout on the twenty-fifth. I started with the earlier date and found a group of signatures with the same name: Montrose.

"A family reunion?" Carlotta said. "A wedding?"

"Not on a Tuesday. More likely a funeral. I bet if we looked it up we'd find an obit with all these names in it." The day after the robbery, half the Montroses were gone and a married couple named Johnson had the only other room. The third day, only one single was occupied by a guest who signed the register as Edward J. Smith of Columbia, South Carolina."

"Do you think that's one of them?" Carlotta said.

"Could be. E. S. – Elton Suggs?"

"Makes sense that he'd rent the room. People might notice a black man taking a room more likely than they would a white one because black men were involved in the robbery."

"If it was Suggs, he stayed in room three-eight." I looked up at the ceiling. "Right over our heads."

XLI

Carlotta and I both like Cajun cooking, and the catfish was exceptional. Payden's kitchen served it up with dirty rice and the vegetable medley you find in every restaurant these days. The restaurant section was another room full of oak and mirrors – and people. It was all but filled, which told me that the Titlow had a steady local clientele. Halfway through the meal, Payden came by our table.

"How's your research going?"

"Slow," I said around a mouthful of rice. "I have to look at every page, examine the signatures and the dates. I should be done by tomorrow."

"I hope you're successful. It wouldn't hurt my business if my B and B has a history. Talk to you later." Every place has a history, dude, I thought. He crossed the room to give a kiss to a pretty brunette and a bro-hug to her companion, a guy who could have passed for Payden's long-lost cousin, right down to the teeth.

I got the impression that Scott and Julie Payden ran the Titlow as some kind of rich kid's hobby and said so.

"Why would you say that, Sam?"

"They're like yuppies I know who decided it would be cool to open a winery and then imported all their grapes and juice from California and have never grown one grape of their own."

"Look at it this way, Sam," Carlotta said, "he employs a lot of people so he doesn't have to do any work himself."

"Spoken like a true member of the proletariat."

She stuck her tongue out at me and went back to her catfish.

We enjoyed mulled wine with cinnamon by the fireplace and around ten o'clock, we went upstairs to the room. The bar's last call was at one, so we decided to wait until three to slip upstairs, figuring that by then everybody on the floor would be asleep and the staff would all have gone home.

I was going to go solo, but Carlotta insisted that she come along. "After all I've been through; I deserve to see the payoff. Besides, how are you going to hold the flashlight, in your teeth?" I didn't argue.

I pulled the plastic sheeting aside and felt the cold drift down from upstairs. No heat. Carlotta went first with the light.

"Walk on the outsides of the treads," I whispered. "Less chance of squeaking."

The third floor was laid out the same as the second, with the stairwell at one end of the hallway and the bath at the other. The floor was swept into piles of sawdust, and a table saw stood beside one of the doors. Lumber and sheetrock were stacked against one wall.

"There's the room."

I was glad the door was unlocked. Sneaking downstairs and swiping a room key from the board behind the registration desk and making it back undetected seemed like a slim prospect at best. I was sure there was a night manager on duty somewhere in the building, but whether he was awake or asleep I had no way of knowing.

Room three-eight was identical to our room below, but without the furniture, it looked a lot bigger. The window sashes were missing, and a sheet of heavy plastic snapped with each gust of wind. The radiator was disconnected and standing in a corner. The black iron steam pipe and fitting hung in the air like an arm with a fist.

Under the window, I saw an area about eight inches by twelve that didn't match the rest of the floor. Sometime in the last century, the radiator must have sprung a leak and rotted the floorboards. The replacement slats were pine, not oak, and had aged to gray over the years. The carpenter used finish nails to tack them in place, so they weren't tongue in groove.

I slipped a chisel into the gap between the old wood and a replacement board. I pushed a little and nothing moved. I slid the flat end of the flooring bar into the gap and tugged with a little more force. The nails groaned, but the board slowly rose.

The rest of them went more easily. I reached into the hole. The floor joists were two-by-tens, rough finished oak. There must have been a lot of it available a hundred years ago. I swept my forearm back and forth, snagging the back of my hand on a nail.

"Anything?"

"Not yet. I'll have to reach my whole arm in." I shucked off my jacket and put my arm in to the shoulder. My fingers hit something soft. A bag of some kind. I got a handful of the fabric and tugged at it. It snagged on a few nails but I was able to haul it out of the opening. It was an old pillowcase. "Got it."

"Uh, Sam…" Carlotta's voice was anything but excited.

"Hello, Dunne."

I rolled into a sitting position and saw a figure in the doorway. It was Tanner. He was holding a satchel in one hand and a gun in the other.

XLII

"How'd you find us?"

"If you look under the back bumper of your van, you'll find the locator I hid there." He gestured with the gun. "Dump it out. Let's see what you've got there."

I upended the pillow case and stacks of banded money bounced on the boards. A lot of it.

"Congratulations, Dunne. You found the buried treasure. Too bad you can't spend it."

"Why? Because you're going to take it away from us?"

He laughed. "Yeah, I am going to take it, but that's not the only reason. Almost all of it's counterfeit."

"What?"

"When Watts and his buddies robbed First National, they made the cashier open a lockbox with a hundred grand in escrow. What they didn't know was somebody switched the real bucks with funny money."

"Your boss, Richard Knight."

"You're smarter than you look, Dunne. He got a tip on a hot stock deal and he uh, 'borrowed' the escrow money. He got counterfeit as a placeholder, he turned a good profit and planned to put it all back a few weeks later, but the robbers came, and the rest you know."

"What's in the bag?"

"A hundred grand in real bills. Knight hired me to find this stash and replace it with real money. The statute of limitations hasn't run out on him yet, and he wants to cover his tracks. But for all the trouble I've been through and the light you shined on me with all your stunts, I think I'll just take both."

"I hate to ask, but what about us?"

"What do you think, Dunne?" He laughed. "By the time anybody finds you two, I'll be in Canada. I'm sure there's somebody across the border who'd be glad to buy good counterfeit paper for fifty cents on the dollar. But before I say goodbye –" His foot lashed out and caught me on the side of my head. He took a step toward me to kick me again.

Carlotta turned off the flashlight.

I rolled away and groped in the dark. I found the flooring bar and swung it at knee level. Tanner gave a grunt of pain and fired at me, but I'd already rolled away. The muzzle flash gave me a good idea where he was, and I whacked his other knee.

I sprang up, and one good shove on those shaky knees sent Tanner into the plastic sheeting over the window casement. The staples gave way with a pop and a rip. I think the word I want is defenestrated. Tanner's last words were "Oh, shit."

I stuck my head through the torn plastic and looked down. Tanner's body was sprawled in the alley below, and beside it looking up at me were Tajc and Blankenship.

Then it was my turn to say, "Oh, shit."

XLIII

"When were you going to tell us, Dunne," Blankenship said. "Or were you just going to send us a postcard from Rio?"

We were sitting by the fireplace in the Titlow. Blankenship and Tajc looking angry, Scott Paden looking totally befuddled, and Carlotta and I looking totally guilty.

I looked to Carlotta. "Do you want to tell them, or should I?"

"Be my guest."

"When you look in the room upstairs, you'll find a hundred grand in real money and a hundred grand in counterfeit. Tanner was hired by a man named Richard Knight who was vice-president of First National Bank when Boley Watts stuck it up. Knight embezzled the cash from an escrow account and put in counterfeit bills as a placeholder. When Boley, the last person who knew where the money was hidden, died, Knight was afraid he'd left some clue to where it was stashed, so he put Tanner on it."

"Keep it coming," Tajc said.

"Tanner tried the nice way first, and when I didn't take the bait, he followed me around for a while. When that didn't work, he threatened Carlotta. Then I understand he got arrested for passing bad bills."

Blankenship said, "But you wouldn't know anything about that, would you, Dunne?"

I shrugged. "Knight had access to counterfeit money once, maybe had some sitting around. I agree, it wouldn't make sense for Knight to double cross his own man. Maybe it was just a coincidence."

"I doubt it, but we'll let that one go for the time being," Blankenship said. "So how did you end up here?"

I told them about the code numbers inside Baby's pickguard. "Boley told me his memory was fading, and he probably stamped the numbers into the metal because he was afraid he'd forget where they hid the loot. Then he had second thoughts and ground them off, but he didn't have time to quite finish the job. Maybe he was interrupted before he could finish; that I don't know.

"Tanner wanted the guitar, figuring it had a map, or some other clue leading to the cash, but it wouldn't have helped him much without the crossword magazines as a reference. It took us a while," I nodded at Carlotta, "but we figured it out. She gets most of the credit."

"So you're saying both of you are going up the river for obstruction?" Tajc said.

"Do you really want that?" I looked from one to the other. "Imagine the headlines: Agents solve 25-year-old cold case, nab embezzler? Do you want that or something like: FBI drops the ball, amateurs score touchdown?"

Tajc bristled. "You cheap punk, I oughta…" He started out of his chair but Blankenship grabbed his arm. "He's got a point, Ralph."

"Is there a reward for the return of the money?"

The question from Carlotta startled the agents. "Yeah, Blankenship said, unless it's been rescinded, there's a five thousand dollar reward for the return of the money. But now that we know it's fake, it's a moot point."

"We can let the lawyers sort that one out," I said. I turned to Payden. "You got your wish, Scott. The Titlow's going to be famous for a lot longer than fifteen minutes." Back to the agents. "So, are we done here?"

"For now," Blankenship said. "We'll need formal statements from you. I'm sure we can rely on you two to cooperate."

"Absolutely." I rose from my chair and held out my hand to Carlotta. "Now, if you'll excuse us, it's been a long night." As we walked away, I turned and said, "By the way, how did you guys know where we are?"

"Should we tell them?" Blankenship said. Tajc just glared. "The E-Z Pass transponder on your windshield. The Pennsylvania Turnpike Commission is very cooperative in federal investigations, unlike some people."

Carlotta and I climbed the stairs, and to borrow a line from "The Most Dangerous Game," I never slept in a better bed.

XLIV

On the drive back to Hanniston, Carlotta was quiet. Finally, I asked, "Something bothering you?"

"Those men who kidnapped me, Sam. I'm afraid for you. What if they have friends who come looking for you?"

"I doubt that would happen. Those two were greedy; I don't think they'd've told anybody what they were up to for fear they'd have to cut them in on the deal. "

"What about the police? What if they find the bodies?"

"Not going to happen." I figured Tiny Settles' men would have shoved Boley's bastard son and his partner under the ice of the Susquehanna. If they were found at all, it wouldn't be until the Spring thaw and twenty miles down the river.

"And I worry about what it's done to you." She hesitated to say it. "Killing someone."

"Wasn't the first time, C." I almost said, "Or the second."

"I know." And she clammed up for the rest of the ride.

XLV

In the end, things turned out better than they might have. Carlotta and I were off the hook with the Feds, and they got the big spotlight for cracking the case. I never heard a word about Carlotta's abductors. For all I know, their bones are still at the bottom of the river someplace. Richard Knight will be going on trial for embezzlement and criminal conspiracy next month. We never did get a reward for finding the money, but Carlotta and I have a standing invitation to stay at the Titlow Hotel any time we want.

Carlotta was a little bit distant with me for a while, but in the end she understood that I did what I had to do to save her life and mine. A little gallantry goes a long way.

Joe Mancini's working on a deal with Boggy Bottom, an indie label that specializes in traditional music, for my prison recording of Boley's blues, and if things go right, it'll hit the charts next spring. *Rolling Stone* is looking at my biography of Eight-String Watts as a possible serialization, and if they don't take it and nobody else wants it, there's always Kindle.

And Baby, what started it all; I still have Boley's handmade masterpiece hanging on the wall in my living room. I've had legitimate offers to buy her, but I think I'll give her to Jorma Kaukonen for his Psylodelic Gallery at the Fur Peace Ranch. Carlotta's right. The Rock'n'Roll Hall of Fame has enough guitars already.

THE END

AFTERWORD:

I always have fun with Sam Dunne stories because as a singer-songwriter myself, I feel such a kinship with the character. I once gave a copy of *Dead Man's Melody* to a woman I met at a book signing. She e-mailed me a few days later and wrote, "I'm a little concerned. How much of you is in this novel?"

The answer? Just enough to know whereof I write.

I owe a special debt to Shirley Dempsey for her insight into the workings of the prison system. The novel would be all the poorer without her invaluable input.

What next for Sam Dunne? Maybe he'll get a call to work the local Renaissance Festival—Murder Most Foul complete with varlets and harlots. It just seems that I'd have a problem getting a hard case like Sam Dunne to wear pantaloons.

ABOUT OUR CREATORS

AUTHOR ·

FRED ADAMS, JR.- is a retired English professor with a lifelong love of pulp fiction. He has created the Hitwolf, Six Gun Terrors, C.O. Jones, Ike Mars, and Sam Dunne series for Airship 27 Productions in addition to contributing to a number of its anthologies. *Dead Man's Melody*, the first of the Sam Dunne series, was nominated as the Best Pulp Novel of the Year in the 2017 Pulp Factory Awards. He describes himself as "living in abject terror of boredom."

INTERIOR ILLUSTRATIONS ·

SAM A. SALAS - has been an artist since the 70's. His first love has always been comics and comic book art. His greatest aspiration was to become a comic book artist with one of the major companies. In the mid 90's Sam and a small band of friends decided to publish his own comics. Thus was born ZUB COMICS. The company published two titles. One was GREAT GALAXIES! A science fiction anthology featuring all original stories with art by Sam. The other title was TELLURIA a fantasy title. In all, the company published 11 books and folded in the early 2000's.

Since then, Sam has done various freelance projects for local independent publishers including several stories for a book titled WICKED AWESOME TALES, and a few stories for Ron Fortier. Now mostly retired, he is always ready to take on new projects and looks forward to working with his friend Ron on this new book.

COVER ARTIST ·

ROB DAVIS - began his professional art career doing illustrations for role-playing games in the late 1980's. Not long after he began lettering and inking, then penciling comics for a number of small black and white comics publishers. At Malibu Comics imprint Eternity Comics Rob gained some notoriety pencilling SCIMIDAR with writer R.A. Jones. Eventually he began working on likeness-intensive comics like TV adaptations of QUANTUM LEAP at Innovation and STAR TREK's DC comics' and was a semi-regular penciler on the DEEP SPACE NINE comics for Malibu. At Marvel he worked on the Saturday morning cartoon adaptation PIRATES OF DARK WATER. After the comics industry implosion in the late 1990's Rob picked up work on video games, advertising illustration and T-shirt design as well as some small press comics like ROBYN OF SHERWOOD for Caliber. Rob continues to do self-published comic book work for his small-press production house REDBUD STUDIO COMICS. Rob is Art Director, Designer and Illustrator for the New Pulp outfit AIRSHIP 27 partnered with writer/editor Ron Fortier. Rob is a two-time recipient of the PULP FACTORY AWARD for "Best Interior Illustrations" for his work on SHERLOCK HOLMES: CONSULTING DETECTIVE. He lives in the wilds of central Missouri with his wife on five and a half acres.

BOOKS BY FRED ADAMS JR.

FRED ADAMS JR. PULP WRITER

SIX-GUN TERRORS Volume One
SIX-GUN TERRORS   Volume Two
SIX-GUN TERRORS Volume Three – The Slithering Terror

HITWOLF
HITWOLF 2 – The Pack

C.O. JONES
C.O. JONES – Skinners
C.O. JONES – The Damned and the Doomed
C.O. JONES- Hometown-U.S.A.

(SAM DUNNE MYSTERIES)
Dead Man's Melody
Blood is the New Black
Strings Attached

(THE SMITH BROTHERS SERIES)
The Eye of Quang Chi

(IKE MARS MYSTERIES)
The Bloody Key
Wired

FANGS OF THE SEA

Find these and other great reading at airship27hangar.com

A FAMILY AFFAIR

When assembling Fred Adams Jr.'s latest Sam Dunne novel, we wanted to maintain some kind of visual unity between it and the two previous Dunne mysteries. Wherein Art Director Rob Davis had used actual items on those compositions (my own hand on the "Dead Man's Melody" and a real camera with pix of a screaming woman for "Blood Is The New Black") the challenge became finding the right item—or prop—for "Strings Attached."

Our "duh" moment came when we realized the plot centered around a famous guitar. Those of you familiar with the series are aware that the protagonist, Sam Dunne, is a working musician. He plays the guitar. So does our son, Kevin. That light bulb moment popped and we rushed to our digital family album where we had several photos of Kevin with a number

of his electric guitars. He loves music, playing, and is quite good. Yes, we're bragging, but what parent doesn't?

So we asked him if he wouldn't mind our tooling one of those pictures for the cover to this title. He was delighted with the idea and seemed more concerned as to which of his guitars would be featured than about the image we would choose. Yup, we told you he is a true musician. So here it is, after Art Director

Rob Davis added some dramatic elements.

Playing the role of Sam Dunne, none other than Kevin Douglas Fortier.

Thanks Kev, we love you.

Dad

Ron Fortier
7/10/2022
Fort Collins, CO

Previous excitement with Sam Dunne:

WHEN THE CURTAIN FALLS

Fifteen years ago Sam Dunne was the lead guitarist and singer for the popular rock band, Gin Sing. Critics and fans prophesied a meteoric rise to the top of the music charts. Then Dunne's bandmates, Eddie Shay and Danny Barton, kicked him to the curb and went chasing after rock stardom without him.

Dunne now works small one night gigs while teaching English Literature at a community college. He's let the past go and learned to accept things as they are. Then he turns the radio on one morning to learn Shay has been murdered: shot to death in his private home studio.

Soon the police start focusing their attention on Dunne as a "person of interest." It's a custom made set-up, with him as the chief suspect based on a fifteen year old grudge he's supposed to be nurturing. When common sense proves to be useless, the former rocker is left with only one recourse: to do his own investigating and find the killer before he's fitted with a prison wardrobe.

Writer Fred Adams Jr. spins a gritty, fascinating mystery authentically set in the world of sex, drugs and rock roll delivering a masterful reading experience along the way. "Dead Man's Melody" is clearly a cut above the rest.

MURDER ON THE SET

Musician Sam Dunne takes on a gig composing a musical score for a cheap, direct to cable slasher film called "Lake Deadly." Much of the film is shot on location around a nearby lake and Dunne soon learns all is not as it seems among the cast and crew. Petty jealousies and hidden animosities threaten to derail the shooting.

What he doesn't imagine is the murder of a young woman on camera. Someone purposely switched out the fake dagger with a real one and the girl's throat is slashed in front of dozen of witnesses. All of it caught on camera.

Once again, Dunne finds himself caught up in a gruesome murder with more than enough suspects to satisfy any weary detective. Only this isn't make believe and as he attempts to solve the mystery, he is well aware the unknown killer may strike again. All are suspects and possible victims at the same time.

For availability of these and other pulp-style reading: *Airship27Hangar.com*

SEAS of HELL

At the height of the Spanish Inquisition, a large number of the faithful fled Spain and the corrupted church to find haven and new lives on a chain of small islands south of Cuba. There, under the guidance of their priest, Father Beppo, they established peaceful fishing villages that would sustain them in both body and soul. It was their small piece of an earthly heaven.

Then black sails appeared on the horizon, furled from the masts of an unholy ship called Votrelec and captained by Varleck, a vampire pirate. Ever on the hunt for fresh bodies to man his crew of the undead, the blood hungry monster is delighted when discovering the unprotected islands. He is overconfident in his dark powers. Soon he realizes the villagers, under the guidance of the old cleric, have no intention of succumbing to his monstrous will. And so the endless battle of good versus evil is joined. But who will emerge victorious and who will fall when the seas run red with blood?

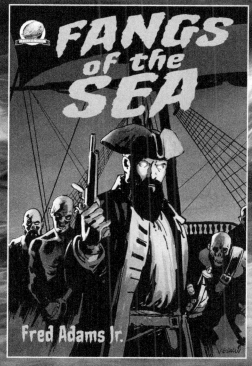

AN AIRSHIP 27 PRODUCTION

PULP FICTION FOR A NEW GENERATION!

AIRSHIP27HANGAR.COM

NEW PULP

Printed in Great Britain
by Amazon

84645644R00081